Cedar River Daydreams

9612

Heartless Hero

Judy Baer

BETHANY HOUSE PUBLISHERS
MINNEAPOLIS, MINNESOTA 55438

Heartless Hero
Copyright © 1997
Judy Baer

Cover illustration by Chris Ellison

Published by Bethany House Publishers
A Ministry of Bethany Fellowship, Inc.
11300 Hampshire Avenue South
Minneapolis, Minnesota 55438
Printed in the United States of America.

Library of Congress Cataloging-in-Publication Data

Baer, Judy.
    Heartless hero / Judy Baer.
       p. cm. — (Cedar River daydreams ; #25)
    Summary: Lexi's younger brother Ben, who has Down's syndrome, becomes the victim of bullies, and while at school Lexi sees her friends tormented by two new students who are bullies, one male and one female.
    ISBN 1–55661–835–2
    [1. Bullies—Fiction. 2. Down syndrome—Fiction. 3. Mentally handicapped—Fiction. 4. High schools— Fiction. 5. School—Fiction 6. Christian life—Fiction.] I. Title. II. Series: Baer, Judy. Cedar River daydreams ; 25.
PZ7.B1395Hf   1996
[Fic]—dc21   96–45908
                                               CIP
                                               AC

For my "horse therapy" friends—
Brenda, Larry, Cocoa, Shazzy,
and all who join us.
It keeps this writer sane!

JUDY BAER received a B.A. in English and Education from Concordia College in Moorhead, Minnesota. She has had over forty novels published and is a member of the National Romance Writers of America, the Society of Children's Book Writers, and the National Federation of Press Women.

Two of her novels, *Adrienne* and *Paige*, have been prizewinning bestsellers in the Bethany House SPRINGSONG series. Both books have been awarded first place for juvenile fiction in the National Federation of Press Women's communications contest.

Chapter One

Lexi Leighton felt like whistling. Or singing. Or skipping. But instead of doing any of those things, she simply gave in to the big grin that was building inside her.

She'd just visted her grandmother at the nursing home.

Sometimes after visiting her, Lexi felt more like crying than smiling. Alzheimer's disease had robbed the elderly woman of her memory—and Lexi of a grandmother. But today had been different. Grandma had been reminiscing about the "good old days" and, for a few moments, had actually seemed to recognize Lexi. It had been wonderful to see that clear light in her eyes.

Grandma had spoken of a time when young men went "courting" a young lady and had to ask her father's permission to marry. Her eyes had glowed when she'd spoken of Lexi's own grandfather, and her gnarled hands had feathered across her face like those of a shy young girl. Lexi had held her hand and laughingly told her of dating practices today. When Grandmother's eyes drifted shut with weariness, Lexi had slipped away.

It had felt both odd and wonderful to get a

glimpse of the woman her grandmother had once been. Lexi determined that she would have to return to the home for another visit very soon.

"Well, hello there, missy," an elderly man in a wheelchair called. "Do you have any fudge today?"

Lexi laughed. "Hi, Mr. Olter. No fudge today."

"Your boyfriend with you?"

"No, Todd's not here."

"It's good to see you anyway," the old man assured her. "But next time bring fudge."

Lexi promised and gave him a peck on the cheek. Since she'd been coming to visit her grandmother, she'd made several friends at the home, Mr. Olter included. Occasionally she and Todd would make a batch of fudge and bring it to the residents. Mr. Olter was her very best customer.

"Going home already?" a shrill voice caught Lexi's attention as she crossed through the reception lounge to the door.

"Hi, Mrs. Witt. Yes. I've already visited my grandmother."

"Good for you." Mrs. Witt wagged a twisted arthritic finger at Lexi. "Next time you come, bring that little brother of yours and his dog."

"Ben and Wiggles? Sure. They love it here."

"And we love them."

Lexi didn't doubt Mrs. Witt for a moment. The people at the nursing home enjoyed seeing young people and pets. They didn't care a bit that Ben had Down's syndrome or that Wiggles wanted to lick everyone on the face. The old people loved them all exactly as they were.

Lexi glanced at her watch and gave a groan. She hadn't planned to stay so long. She'd promised to help her mother cook dinner. Ever since Mrs. Leighton had been diagnosed with multiple sclerosis, Lexi had tried to do what she could—occasionally cleaning, cooking, and running errands. Her mother was doing amazingly well with very few episodes of the illness. Still, Lexi *liked* helping her mother. She was even getting to be a fairly good cook!

Hurrying, she stretched her long, slender legs into a lope and felt fingers of afternoon air ruffle her dark blond hair. Intent on deciding whether she should offer to make pudding, hot fudge topping for ice cream, or a cake for dessert, Lexi almost didn't notice the sounds of fighting until she turned the corner to the street her house was on. Finally, however, the crying and yelling pierced her consciousness. She looked up, scanning the neighborhood for the location of the trouble.

It was coming from her own backyard!

"Babies, babies, stinky little babies! Is that all you two can do? Play with dollies in the sandbox?"

"We're not babies!" an upsettingly familiar voice shouted.

"Are too. Big fat babies! You still play with blocks!"

"Quit it!" another familiar voice cried.

"*You* quit it. Grow up." The smacking sound of something hitting flesh carried through the air.

"Owwww!" Lexi's brother Ben sobbed. Wiggles' frantic barking turned into a howl as loud as that of his master.

"Watch it!" That was Thomas Watkins' voice. Thomas had recently moved into the neighborhood and sometimes came over to the Leightons to build elaborate cities of snap-together blocks in the sand-box with Ben. "You're gonna hurt him."

"You're a bigger baby than he is," the harsh voice taunted, "'cause your brain isn't broken like his and you still play this way."

"Maybe he's retarded too," another voice speculated with a jeer. "Two big dumb babies!"

Lexi's feet flew over the pavement. She took a shortcut across the neighbor's yard and burst onto the scene behind her own house just as two older boys dodged between some shrubs and disappeared. Lexi could see the back of their jean jackets and the waffled bottoms of their tennis shoes, but nothing more.

She increased her speed and dived through the bushes after them. "Wait a minute! Stop. Come back here!"

When the boys turned to look at her, she recognized their faces. They were from the middle school near the Academy, a special school for handicapped children. One boy had bright red hair, the other dusty blond. She would not forget the disdainful looks on their faces.

She might have caught them if a city bus hadn't come by at that moment. The doors opened and the devious pair jumped in. By the time Lexi reached the bus stop, the lumbering vehicle was pulling away.

Flushed and furious, she hurried home, where she could still hear Wiggles barking and Benjamin crying. Thomas was crying too, Lexi discovered, but his sobs were silent. Tears streamed down his face as he gulped great swallows of air. Though Thomas was older than Ben, he certainly didn't look it. He was small and pale with a pinched mouth and high cheekbones.

Thomas was usually very quiet. He seemed content to entertain Benjamin with elaborate constructions in the sandbox. It had surprised Lexi that Thomas didn't seek out boys his own age, but now that she'd gotten a glimpse of what the boys that age were capable of, she didn't blame Thomas. She didn't like them either.

By this time, Mrs. Leighton was in the yard, heading for the crying pair. Even though the danger was past, neither Thomas nor Ben seemed able to quit crying.

"What happened?" Mrs. Leighton asked sharply of Lexi.

"I just caught the tail end of it. Two boys from the middle school—a redhead and a blonde—were taunting and teasing Ben and Thomas. They were calling them 'babies' and 'retarded' and lobbing things through the air at them." Lexi picked up a plastic block. "These."

Mrs. Leighton's mouth set in a tight line. She gathered both boys to her for a hug before efficiently dusting them off. Then she spoke in a light, soothing voice. "It's okay. They're gone. Come in the house and we'll get you cleaned up. You must be thirsty after such an experience. Let's get some lemonade, and I want to hear all about it."

Ben's head bobbed in agreement. Even Thomas let himself be led willingly into the Leighton house under Mrs. Leighton's motherly arm. Lexi glanced at the elaborate city, now in ruins, that the boys had built. It was hardly something built by "babies." Angrily, she turned and walked toward the house.

Thomas's jacket was lying on the grass. Lexi bent to pick it up. It was small, almost smaller than Ben's own jacket. Thomas was taller and lighter than Ben, who had broad shoulders. A penlight fell out of the pocket. Lexi caught it before it hit the ground, and a wave of sadness washed over her. She could just imagine the bookish, introverted Thomas studying some bug or leaf with the little flashlight. And she could imagine how stupid the rougher, more physical boys would think that was.

Children could be so cruel! Innocent, trusting Ben and frail, timid Thomas had done nothing to deserve the onslaught of nastiness that had been turned on them. She looked at the little penlight. Thomas was obviously more of a scholar than a fighter. A dork. A wimp. A boy the other boys didn't respect. Lexi recognized it from her own time in middle school. There was always a child or two more timid and shy than the rest. They were usually young for their age and not "sophisticated" in the ways of "almost" teens. For whatever reason, those kids always attracted the bullies and the teasing, the taunts and the jeers. It was as though there were certain types of kids who always turned out to be victims, the butt of jokes, the laughing-stock of the class. That was what Thomas made Lexi think of—the little victim of every bully in school.

Mrs. Leighton had the boys cleaned up and at the table when Lexi entered. Both had huge glasses of lemonade in front of them, and on the table a plate of cookies that could have fed an entire football team. The jean-clad Mrs. Leighton was wiping her damp hands on a dish towel. She looked up as Lexi came in.

At that moment, Ben gave a loud hiccup. It startled all of them, especially Ben, who in spite of his tears, began to laugh. Thomas, his face a sad picture, turned to Ben with a surprised expression. Even his lips twisted upward in a small smile.

"Crying gives you the hiccups, doesn't it, Ben?" Mrs. Leighton observed.

"Those boys were mean, Mom," Ben said righteously. "They *made* me cry. And me and Thomas weren't doing *nuthin'* to them!"

"You and Thomas weren't doing anything to them," Mrs. Leighton corrected gently.

"That's what I said."

Mrs. Leighton let it pass.

Ben, however, wanted to describe in detail what had just happened outside.

"We were building our school," he explained. "Right, Thomas?"

Thomas nodded. His pale hair was dusty and tousled. Lexi thought she'd never seen a more pitiful-looking child.

"And they sneaked up on us and started hitting us with blocks and calling us babies. I'm not a baby, am I, Mom?"

"Not at all, Benjamin."

"Thomas, Ben, did you know those boys?" Lexi asked.

"I've seen them before, but I don't know their names," Thomas whispered. He rubbed his eye with the back of his hand. "Can I go home now?"

"Let us go with you. Ben, can you play in Thomas's backyard while we visit with his mother?"

They walked Thomas the few steps to his back door. Mrs. Leighton knocked on it as Ben settled himself on the porch with a box of miniature cars.

Mrs. Watkins appeared startled to see the threesome at the door. She was a thin, nervous woman with pale eyes and hair that was pulled away from her face with a thick barrette. "Thomas? Mrs. Leighton? Is everything all right?"

Lexi noticed a quaver of fear in her voice. Had she seen the bullies picking on the boys and not done something about it?

"We'd like to talk to you." Mrs. Leighton pushed Thomas forward. His mother stepped aside, signaling them to come in.

Lexi had not been in the house since the Watkinses had moved in a few weeks ago. It was immaculate. A cake was cooling on the counter. An old school photo of Thomas hung on the refrigerator revealing that in spite of his still-small size, Thomas *had* grown since the picture was taken.

As the two women engaged in the social small talk that adults usually do before getting down to the issue at hand, Lexi thought about Thomas.

He'd seemed lonely from the day the moving truck arrived with the Watkins' furniture. She'd seen him wander through the yard and house as if he were lost until he spotted Ben and Wiggles in their backyard.

Ben, who had no friends from his school nearby, was delighted that the new boy in the neighborhood was willing to play with him. They tossed a ball that first day and spent time in the sandbox building roads for Thomas's vast miniature car collection. After that, Thomas showed up on the Leightons' doorstep nearly every afternoon to play with Ben.

At first it had been worrisome to Lexi's parents. They were afraid that once Thomas was settled in school with students who were not handicapped, he would lose interest in Benjamin and abandon him. It had happened before, and Ben had been devastated, unable to understand why his "friend" no longer wanted to be with him. So far, however, that hadn't happened.

Instead, Ben and Thomas's friendship had blossomed. Bookish Thomas was both patient and kind with Ben, and Ben thought Thomas was the greatest playmate in the world. Both seemed to benefit from the other's companionship.

"Thomas, have you been crying?" Mrs. Watkins asked as she noticed the red rims around her son's eyes. "What's happened?"

"Some boys were picking on Thomas and Ben," Lexi said. "They were calling them names and throwing stuff at them. I chased them away, but we thought you should know. . . ."

"Oh no!" Mrs. Watkins gasped. She grew even more pale—if that was possible. "It's started *already!*"

Then, as if remembering her son was present, Mrs. Watkins reached out to ruffle his hair. "Thomas, go upstairs and take a shower. You'll feel better. Those clothes look as though most of the backyard came in with them. We'll have a snack when you come down."

Thomas's head bobbed and he disappeared, obviously relieved to be dismissed.

"What's started?" Mrs. Leighton asked, picking

up on the odd comment Mrs. Watkins had made. This was hardly the response she'd expected.

"I'd hoped to see the last of them," Mrs. Watkins said wearily, "but apparently it won't be any better here."

"What do you mean?"

Mrs. Watkins indicated that Lexi and her mother should sit down. She wrung her hands together in a knot as she explained. "Maybe it's Thomas's physical size. He's small for his age and not terribly athletic. Or perhaps it's the fact that he loves to read and learn rather than to hit a ball and run. Anyway, it seems that something in Thomas brings the worst out in some children."

"Bullies," Lexi blurted. She was remembering that she, too, had thought Thomas seemed vulnerable, an easy target.

"Yes. There are certain personality types that seem to attract more negative attention than others, I suppose. Thomas is sweet and bright but also timid and underdeveloped for his age."

"Which makes him a perfect target for a bully," Mrs. Leighton concluded, "because bullies pick on people to prove how strong they are, to make themselves feel bigger and better."

She put her hand on Mrs. Watkins' trembling one. "We understand. Because our son has Down's syndrome, we've dealt with bullies for a long time. They're too immature and childish to pick on children of their own age, size, or capabilities—so they pick on children like Ben."

"I suppose that's why Thomas enjoys Ben. They have something in common," Mrs. Watkins said. "He's acted almost *relieved* to have Ben next door.

He's very fond of him already."

"It's hard not to be fond of Ben," Mrs. Leighton said with a smile. "Bullies rule with fear and threats. Ben doesn't know anything about any of those."

"I think some of the most hurtful teasing has been from children Thomas considered friends. They would pretend they didn't mean any harm by the hurtful words they'd say. I never believe the words 'just teasing' anymore. If your feelings have been hurt, you've been bullied."

"Girls can be pretty bad at stuff like that," Lexi added. "But they usually use words rather than physical stuff to bully each other."

"Threats and intimidation," Mrs. Leighton finished. "How well I know! You would come home crying if some little girl told you she wouldn't talk to you or be your friend unless you did as she asked. We all need to have friends and to be loved. It's pretty scary when people threaten to take that away."

"I've been afraid that sometime someone would try to get Thomas to do something dangerous to prove he could be part of a group," Mrs. Watkins admitted. Tears filled her eyes. "The last two years have been so hard—for all of us."

She wiped away the tears and squared her shoulders. "That's why we were so happy to move here. We thought it would be a clean start for Thomas." Her voice cracked. "But the trouble has started again already. . . ."

Thomas returned at that moment, freshly scrubbed and looking slightly less dismal. Mrs. Leighton and Lexi quickly said their good-byes.

———

Ben was no longer in the Thomas's backyard, and Dr. Leighton's vehicle was in the driveway.

"Dad's home," Lexi observed. "He's going to be upset when we tell him about this."

Lexi's prediction was correct. When they entered the kitchen, Ben and his father were sitting face-to-face across the kitchen table. Ben was looking anxious as he repeated the story of the incident with Thomas and the bullies. Dr. Leighton's face was tight with concern. He looked up as Lexi and her mother came in.

"I see Ben's already told you," Mrs. Leighton said. She smoothed her son's thick dark hair as she sat down next to him.

"Lexi, do you know these children?"

"Not personally, but I think I've seen them around. They're from the middle school."

"Ben, do you know *why* these boys were mean to you?" Dr. Leighton asked.

Ben blinked innocently. "Because I'm a big dumb baby?"

The muscle in Dr. Leighton's jaw worked. "You are *not* a 'big dumb baby'!"

"They said so. We weren't mean to them, Dad. Really."

"Of course you weren't. You and Thomas are great little boys. Bullies are cowards. They pick on people they know won't hurt them."

"They scared us, Dad. Me and Thomas." The tears he'd been holding back flooded Ben's eyes. "They said they were gonna 'get' us. What does that mean?"

"Have you seen these boys around Benjamin before, Lexi?"

"No. Actually, I don't think they were really after Ben. I think Thomas is the one who attracted them to this neighborhood."

Mrs. Leighton picked up the story and told her husband what Mrs. Watkins had said.

"It seems that poor Thomas can't get away from older, bigger boys picking on him. He's very vulnerable. Bullies can sense that sort of thing just like sharks can sense blood in the water."

Benjamin began to squirm in his chair. "Can I play with Wiggles now?"

"You don't want to talk about this anymore, do you, buddy?" Dr. Leighton ruffled his hair. "Go on."

The child's expression grew apprehensive. "I don't have to go outside, do I?"

"Wiggles likes it outside."

"But I don't. Not now."

"You can take him to your room if you like."

With a little whoop of delight, Ben was off the chair and calling the dog.

When he was out of hearing distance, Mrs. Leighton gave a huge sigh. "Now we have a child who's afraid to go outside. What are we going to do?"

"I'm not sure yet, but we'll do something."

Lexi was startled by the forcefulness of her father's statement. He was furious—as furious as she'd ever seen him, and now that Ben was out of the room he was letting it show.

"Dad?" she said tentatively. "Are you okay?"

"Not really. This is very troublesome to me."

"The boys can play in the basement for a while,"

Mrs. Leighton offered. "Maybe that old saying 'Out of sight, out of mind' will apply and those children will leave us alone."

"It's not that easy," Dr. Leighton said. "Believe me, I know."

Both Lexi and Mrs. Leighton looked at him curiously.

Dr. Leighton smiled weakly. "You'd never know it to look at me now, but I was a very scrawny little kid."

"I remember Grandma talking about it," Lexi offered. "She said you 'took your time filling out.'"

"That was putting it kindly. I looked like a bird next to most of the boys in my class—and the girls were taller yet!"

"Well, you grew out of it," Mrs. Leighton said with a smile. Her husband was six foot two and athletic. He played both racquetball and squash and ran five miles a day whenever his schedule allowed.

"Not soon enough. I can identify with poor Thomas. I was the target for every bully in my class during grade school and junior high." A muscle jumped in Dr. Leighton's cheek. "First it was name-calling, then pushing and shoving. You name it, I experienced it."

"What did you do?" Lexi was horrified to think that her big, strong father had suffered in this way.

Her father chuckled ruefully. "Something that not every kid can do—I grew. And grew. And grew. I left eighth grade a scrawny little runt and entered ninth almost a foot taller. My growth hormones just kicked in. I was taller than any of the boys who'd been harassing me. By the time I was a sophomore, I'd filled out sufficiently to play football. I was good at it too. Good practice dodging all those bullies for so many years, I suppose. Bullies are weak and cowardly. No one was going to pick on someone who could actually hurt them if they chose."

"So nature took care of your problem," Lexi concluded.

"Exactly."

"I'm not sure that's going to happen for either Thomas or Ben."

"I realize that."

"So what can we do?" Mrs. Leighton asked worriedly.

Dr. Leighton considered the question. "Frankly, Ben will be easier to protect than Thomas. His school environment is the Academy. We can talk to the administration there and make sure that the students know that bullying is inappropriate behavior. I think we can and should shield Ben from some of what Thomas will still experience."

"Maybe I should have one of the guys from school teach him to fight," Lexi said indignantly.

"*Not* a good idea," Dr. Leighton said. "The kids being bullied really are smaller and weaker than the bullies who pick on them. Their chances of losing the fight—or getting hurt—are high."

"Besides, Lexi, that's not the kind of role model we want," Mrs. Leighton murmured. "I can imagine that fighting back could even encourage a bully to torment someone more."

"What then?"

"Bullies seek out the weakest, most vulnerable, most victimlike subjects. I didn't realize until I'd grown so much and could intimidate the boys who'd once intimidated me that it wasn't *size* I lacked—it was self-confidence. If Ben and Thomas act confident and unworried when they are harassed, I doubt that most bullies will persist too long. It's no fun to bully someone who isn't bothered by their antics. In my mind, bullies are kids who don't have enough to do. Maybe this neighborhood or the middle school needs more recreational activities."

"Would any of this have helped you when you were a kid?" Lexi asked.

Dr. Leighton's expression darkened as if a bad memory had entered his thoughts. "Helped *me*? I can't say. Sometimes I thought I'd been burdened with my own personal tormentor—Arlon Henning."

"Arlon Henning?" Lexi giggled. "His name doesn't sound so tough."

"Don't be fooled by that. He was nastiness personified. Whatever I had, Arlon wanted. First it was baseball cards and cat's-eye marbles. Later it was my baseball glove. Even in high school, Arlon was a pain. He made sure he dated every single girl I asked out. If he couldn't steal or 'borrow' what I had, he'd go out and buy one just like it—only better."

"He sounds awful."

"When I think about it now, he was probably jealous of everything I had. Arlon had a lot of brothers and sisters. I doubt he got much attention at home. I also remember my friends telling me that Arlon was pretty rotten at home too. His mother would ask him to do something and Arlon would act as if he hadn't heard her. She'd ask again and he'd ignore her. She'd threaten to punish him and he'd act as if she weren't even in the room. Finally, after a big yelling scene, Arlon's mother would fly off the handle entirely. Sometimes she would punish him terribly. Other times, she'd just throw her hands in the air and give up."

"But what does that have to do with bullying?" Lexi asked.

"I would imagine sometimes Arlon *got away* with his defiance, right?" Mrs. Leighton asked. She seemed to understand where her husband was going with his story.

"Exactly. So Arlon figured out that if he ignored his mother enough, he could get out of work. He figured he could put up with his mother's inconsistent behavior more easily than do the work she'd asked him to do. And if his own *mother* treated him unfairly and unpredictably, why shouldn't everyone else? Arlon always made sure he was unfair and unpredictable *first*."

"Sounds as though you understand him pretty well, Dad."

"I've had a lot of years to think about it. Arlon and I graduated together almost twenty-five years ago, and there's not a year that goes by that something doesn't remind me of Arlon."

Lexi was surprised at how strongly her father still felt about this old classmate. Twenty-five years was a long time, and yet when her dad talked about Arlon Henning, it seemed as though he were talking about things that happened only yesterday!

Was that how poor Thomas was going to remember his life someday? Lexi was pretty sure he wasn't going to grow up to be as big, strong, handsome, or smart as her dad. Maybe Thomas would be a bully's victim all his life.

Chapter Two

"Anybody home?" Binky McNaughton peeked her head around the corner of the Leightons' back door. Her curious little face wreathed in smiles when she saw Lexi at the dining room table in front of her sewing machine.

"Come on in. I need a break," Lexi invited.

"Peggy, Jennifer, and Angela are with me."

"Well, don't leave them outside!" Lexi pushed away the scrap of fabric she was working on. She sighed and ran her fingers through her hair. "I'm glad you're here. I was about to start screaming."

"What are you making?" Angela Hardy asked. Her dark eyes were wide as she studied the multi-colored scraps of cloth spread across the table. Angela had pale skin and shoulder-length hair that gleamed in the light. With a quick move of her hands she scraped her long bangs out of her eyes.

"Looks like *doll* clothes," Jennifer Golden said with a hint of a sneer as she held up a small chunk of fabric. "Nothing that would fit a *human*." Fit and athletic looking, Jennifer had little time for the fussy detail work for which Lexi had so much patience. She gave the gum she was chewing a huge pop. "You haven't reverted to playing with Barbies, have you?"

Lexi grabbed the bright piece of floral cloth out of her friend's hand. "I'm making a quilt, you un-informed people. It's going to be gorgeous—if it doesn't drive me crazy first. I got the pattern from the craft lady at the nursing home. She says the residents love to make this design." She sighed. "I guess those ladies have had a lot more experience at this than me."

"What's it for?" Jennifer asked.

"My bed. I want to make a dust ruffle and pillow shams too, but at the rate I'm going, I'll be out of college by the time it's done."

"Lexi, you're the only person I've ever known who actually makes *bedding*! Isn't that what stores are for?" Jennifer blurted.

"I think it's neat," Angela defended her friend. "And it's going to be very pretty"—she eyed the col-orful mess—"if it ever gets done."

"Why aren't you sewing clothes, as usual?" Binky inquired. "They look easier."

"Nothing is easy today." Lexi pushed away from the table. "How about some lemonade?"

"Now you're talking," Jennifer responded. "Any cookies available?"

When the girls were settled in the living room with a healthy supply of food and beverages, Lexi finally asked, "What's up? Why did you come over?"

"Big news. Really big. HUGE." Binky's bright eyes danced. "We heard it at the mall."

"A sale at Shoes and Such? Two for the price of one at Record City? Free burritos with a pop in the food court?"

Binky snorted. "That's not news."

"Binky's right," Angela said. "This is pretty interesting."

"Then *tell* me!"

"Roger Mason has moved to Cedar River!" All three girls gave squeals of excitement.

"Huh?" Lexi stared at them blankly. "Who is Roger Mason? And what's the big deal about him?"

"Who *is* he?" Jennifer nearly yelled. "Just Mr. Football, that's all, named by the Sportscasters Association. He's already got scholarship offers from half a dozen colleges. He's been written up on the sports pages ever since he was a freshman in high school. *Now* do you know who Roger Mason is?"

"Oh, him." Lexi remained unimpressed. "I thought he already went to school somewhere near here."

"He did, but he decided that he wanted to play for a bigger school, so his parents moved to Cedar River," Angela said.

"Really?" Lexi looked surprised. "Just so he could play football?"

"He plays basketball and runs track too. Cedar River's sports program just got a big boost." Jennifer looked triumphant. She liked following Cedar River High's athletic teams.

"I didn't think they were too bad before," Lexi said quietly. "Todd's on the team. And lots of other great guys."

"I'm not saying they aren't good. It's just that Roger Mason is *outstanding*. I heard the coaches are so happy they're doing handstands. Coach Drummond can't quit grinning."

Lexi picked thoughtfully at a bit of thread on the leg of her jeans. "Fine, but I think our guys will do great with or without this Roger fellow."

"Oh, Lexi, you're so loyal," Binky said. "We're not saying our teams are bad. They're pretty good. But with Roger's help, maybe we can turn a good season into a great one! Wouldn't it be fun to go to state tournaments? We could rent a motel room and get a pass for all the games and eat in restaurants. . . ."

"What do you care more about?" Jennifer asked. "The games or the food?"

"It's not that I don't like the games. . . ."

Everyone burst out laughing. Binky and her brother Egg were skinny as car antennas and ate like they were always starved.

"Besides," Binky said haughtily, "I know Roger Mason personally."

"You didn't tell us that!" Angela exclaimed. "How? When?"

"It was a long time ago," Binky admitted. "Grade school. Roger's family lived in Cedar River once before. He went to the same grade school as Egg and I did."

"Wow, then you have a real connection," Jennifer observed. "You'll have to renew your old friendship. Wouldn't that get Minda mad!"

She referred to Minda Hannaford, self-appointed fashion guru for their high school and leader of a clique of snobbish girls who called themselves the High Fives. Minda and Jennifer were not usually on friendly terms. Of course, Minda was seldom on friendly terms with anyone outside her chosen circle of friends.

Binky looked uncertain, as if something Jennifer had said made her uncomfortable. "I didn't know him *that* well. . . ."

"What about Egg? I'll bet they played together." Angela sometimes dated Egg and was always interested in everything about his life before they'd met.

"Noooo, not really." There was an odd tone in Binky's voice.

"Was he nice?" Peggy sounded interested.

Binky didn't answer. Instead she became deeply engrossed in following the crease in her khakis with her index finger. It was a long time before she looked up. The other girls were staring at her.

"Well?" they demanded. "Was he?"

"Nice? Not exactly." Binky sounded as though she were trying to swallow the words.

"What's that supposed to mean?" Angela asked.

"I guess I shouldn't have bragged about knowing him," Binky admitted. "I didn't know him well—except that I knew enough to stay away from him."

"Huh?" Jennifer looked totally befuddled.

"Roger was a big bully back in grade school."

"Did he tease you?" Lexi asked.

"That and worse. Sometimes he really pounded on the boys—especially Egg." She looked thoughtful. "I suppose it had something to do with his size. He was big even back then. He thought everyone should listen to him and do what he said. He was big enough to make them do it."

"He doesn't sound very nice," Angela said.

"Actually," Binky said, "he was really *mean*."

Then her eyes brightened. "But I'm sure he's grown out of that by now! Kids do. He's probably the sweetest guy in the world. Why shouldn't he be? Everything is going his way—scholarships, starring athlete, fame, glory. He's probably a big old teddy bear by now! Besides, he never really did pick much on me. Only Egg."

"This guy was that mean to Egg?" Angela sounded shocked.

Binky gave a resigned sigh as if they were tearing the whole story out of her bit by painful bit. "Egg wasn't a very good-looking little kid. You know, goofy looking."

No one spoke. No one wanted to say that Egg was *still* a little goofy looking with his gangly body and big Adam's apple.

"He had great big feet and huge ears. His head has kind of grown into his ears now and you can hardly notice it, but when he was little . . . whew!" Binky looked a little ashamed. "I got punished once for calling him *Dumbo*."

"Binky!"

"He called me an old maid," Binky defended herself. "I didn't know what it meant but it sounded awful. I didn't do anything worse than that!"

"Get on with the story," Jennifer commanded. "We haven't got all year."

"Egg bugged Roger, that's all."

"What about him?"

"Everything, I guess. The fact that Egg even existed. We didn't call Egg by his nickname then. Everybody called him Edward—except Roger, of course. He called him *Worm*."

"Nice guy," Peggy said sarcastically.

"He really hurt Egg's feelings. He'd steal Egg's lunch at school and dip it into the toilet before handing it back to him."

"Oh, gross!" Angela looked as if she wanted to gag.

"He'd color on Egg's desk and on Egg's art pictures that hung on the wall." Binky's eyes clouded. "Once he used scissors to cut a hole in Egg's new winter coat. That was bad. Mom and Dad didn't have money to buy a new one, so Egg's new coat had to be patched after the first day he'd worn it."

"This guy sounds like a real horror show," Jennifer muttered. "What was his point?"

"Roger was lots bigger than Egg. He was cute too. All the girls liked him. Of course, they liked Egg too, because everybody does." Binky considered her statement. "Maybe that's why Roger didn't like Egg. He didn't want anybody else to be as popular as he was."

"There's no one sweeter than Egg," Angela said with sincerity.

"At first Mom and Dad thought we were exaggerating about the way Roger treated him." Binky's brow furrowed. "Come to think about it, they *always* thought we were exaggerating."

"That's because you usually are," Jennifer said under her breath.

"I heard that!" Binky made a face at her friend but continued with her story. "It wasn't until Egg came home with the hole in his new jacket that they started to believe us."

"What did they do?" Lexi wanted to know.

"Nothing. Roger moved right after that."

"And hopefully he grew up," Peggy said.

"I've known lots of mean little kids that turned out all right," Lexi offered.

"Nobody can stay that rotten," Jennifer concluded. "Maybe it's a good thing he got it out of his system. He's probably a great guy now."

Binky's expression cleared. "Right. And it's really cool that he's here to play football."

Jennifer stood up. "Come on, let's go tell the guys."

"Hey, Mike!" Jennifer yelled as they neared the garage. Mike Winston, a taller, slightly darker version of his younger brother Todd, stood in the doorway of the garage he owned and operated. "Have you got good help in there?"

"Sure, Ed's here." Mike referred to Ed Bell, his assistant.

"I meant Todd, Egg, and . . ."

"But you said *good* help. That's Ed." Mike grinned and tipped his head toward the back of the shop. "They're over there."

"How's school?" Lexi inquired. Mike was taking a night class at the junior college these days, something he'd begun after the death of his fiancée. Nancy had died of AIDS, the disease she'd contracted long before she and Mike had met. After that, Mike had been searching for ways to keep busy and his mind occupied.

"I should have gone to college right after high school," Mike admitted. "I think it would have been easier. It's really tough to get back in the habit of studying after being away from it for a few years. Still, it's worth it. I'm learning a lot."

"Someday he'll be smart like me," Ed said with a grin as he approached the girls, wiping his hands on a greasy cloth. "I'm reading Shakespeare, you know."

"No kidding?" Lexi was amazed. "For real?"

" 'Romeo, Romeo, wherefore art thou, Romeo?' " Ed quoted.

When he'd first come to Mike's garage he'd been secretive and insecure, all due to the fact that he couldn't read. Once Lexi and the gang had figured out what Ed was hiding, they'd all encouraged him to find a tutor. Now he devoured books like they were candy for the mind. He was reading authors and topics he'd never dreamed he'd be able to understand.

"I'm impressed!" Lexi beamed. "You are totally amazing."

"Nah, I just have a good tutor, that's all. In fact, she's so good that she says pretty soon I'll be able to tutor others who can't read. Great, huh?"

"Who gave you time off to brag?" Mike asked. "Is that transmission done yet?"

"Not yet, boss." Ed winked at the girls, saluted toward Mike, and sauntered away while stuffing the greasy rag in the back pocket of his coveralls.

"Aren't you going to talk to us?" Todd shouted from the back. His dark blue eyes warmed under his thatch of blond hair as he looked at Lexi. Todd, Egg, Jerry Randall, Matt Windsor, and Tim Anders were circling the front end of an old car with the hood open.

"What's going on back here, surgery?" Jennifer asked.

"Oil change and tune up," Egg said. "Todd's showing us how."

"Showing *you* how. The rest of us already have that information," Jerry corrected. Dark haired and good-looking, Jerry never missed an opportunity to point out that he had superior knowledge. Sometimes his cockiness was hard to take, but Egg and

Todd usually ignored it, as they did now.

Matt, who wore a black leather jacket and an earring, never took his eyes from the motor. Tim Anders, a thin, pleasant guy who only occasionally hung out with the others, shifted from one foot to the other and looked as though he didn't know quite what to say.

"What are you doing here?" Egg asked. "I thought you were doing . . . girl stuff."

"That's a sexist remark if I've ever heard one," Jennifer retorted. "We could be changing oil in a car too, you know. That *is* 'girl stuff' these days."

"Yeah, Binky keeps reminding me that I'm 'politically incorrect,' " Egg said with a put-on sigh. "But what *are* you doing here?"

"We came to tell you the big news," Jennifer enthused. She spilled out the story of Roger Mason and his heroic return to Cedar River.

"No kidding?" Jerry was impressed. "I've read a lot about him. He's supposed to be great. College scholarships all over the place. If he keeps on the way he's been going, he's bound to be a draft pick for professional football someday."

Tim and Matt began to discuss Roger's skill on the field while Todd asked a number of questions. The only one who didn't seem enthused about the news was Egg.

He'd become very quiet as Jennifer spoke, frown lines burrowing deep into his brow. The more the others talked, the more worried Egg seemed to get.

Chapter Three

"La . . . la . . . la . . . Ouch! You dropped that music stand on my foot!" Binky glared at her brother as Egg scrambled to right the stand he'd been fumbling with.

The music room was in normal chaos as the students warmed up for chorus. The director, Mrs. Waverly, was a popular teacher, and her classes were always full.

Lexi, Peggy, and Jennifer jockeyed for their positions while the boys did the same. Mrs. Waverly glanced up from her music and put a finger over her lips. Her hair, piled on top of her head, sprouted several pencils, and her kind eyes twinkled with amusement at her students. The din subsided as students found their places and pulled out their sheet music. Then a buzz of whispered conversation began to hum throughout the room.

"There they are!" Lexi heard Gina hiss.

Lexi turned to see who "they" might be.

It was obvious that the newest students in Cedar River High had arrived.

Roger Mason was huge. He had to be at least six foot three, Lexi guessed. With meaty hands and oversized feet clad in gigantic tennis shoes, Roger looked like a giant compared to the other guys in the room. No wonder coach Drummond was excited about having him play for CRH. He was practically a football team all by himself!

His sandy brown hair was sprouting a half-grown-out buzz cut and his blue eyes were pale as ice chips. Surprising for one so muscular and massive, Roger's face was round, almost moon-shaped, his cheeks puffy with what Lexi's mom would call "baby fat." A thick roll of soft, excess poundage also hung over his belt.

He swaggered as he walked, lighter on his feet than could be expected for his size.

"He's awesome!" Gina gasped. "Look at those arms and legs!"

If size were the only judge, Lexi mused, Roger Mason *was* definitely awesome. Still, she didn't like the narrowness or close-set stance of his eyes, or the lip that curled as he observed the room.

"And how about the girl?" Jerry whispered. "Va-vavoom!"

Lexi had hardly noticed the girl until she insinuated herself around Roger's massive hulk and stood in front of him. She was tall and thin as a rail. Her red-brown hair—obviously from a bottle—was styled and fixed with hairspray. A row of five pierced earrings marched up the edge of one ear. Her face, thin almost to the point of gaunt, was pretty. Her features were sharp, especially her nose, and her narrow lips were highlighted with deep burgundy. The make-up, expertly applied, made her skin look flawless and porcelain. When she lifted her hand to put it on Roger's arm, Lexi noticed that her fingernails were painted navy blue.

"She's driving back and forth to school every day," Gina hissed, "just to be with *him*."

"Roger Mason and Cindy Jarvis?" Mrs. Waverly consulted a memo slip from the front office. "Welcome to chorus."

Roger acknowledged the teacher with a tip of his head. Cindy said nothing.

"Bass, I presume?" Mrs. Waverly asked.

Roger nodded.

"Then you may sit in that section. Todd, move over one seat, please." Then Mrs. Waverly looked at Cindy. "And you?"

"Soprano."

"Then you may sit on this end. Anna Marie, make room, please."

As the students shuffled about, Lexi studied the new pair. No confidence lacking in either one of them, she decided. They behaved as if entering a new school were the easiest thing in the world. Lexi thought back to the time when *she* was the new girl in town. Her attitude had been quite different.

"Students, please say hello to our newest chorus members, Roger and Cindy."

Dutifully, everyone mouthed, "Hello, Roger. Hello, Cindy." Egg McNaughton was the only one whose lips didn't move.

"They act as if they *deserve* all this attention," Gina huffed. "They really think they are big deals, don't they?"

Lexi shot Gina a startled glance. She was surprised that Gina would notice. After all, the High Fives usually acted the same way.

Mrs. Waverly didn't allow any more time for speculation. She tapped her baton on the edge of her music stand. "Turn to page twelve in the blue book. After warm-ups, I want to start a new piece."

Roger was disinterested in the music, Lexi observed. He made only a token effort to participate. By the time Mrs. Waverly got to announcements at the end of the class period, he was practically asleep.

"Those of you who are Emerald Tones must remember that you have an extra practice this week. You're singing for the Commercial Club luncheon next Thursday. I will arrange for passes to excuse you from school for that hour and also for transportation. Bring your green blazers Thursday morning and store them in my office. Is that clear?"

"What's the Emerald Tones?" Roger was awake and sitting forward in his chair, looking curious. The phrase "passes to excuse you from school" must have done it.

"It's our swing choir," Mrs. Waverly explained. "We sing not only for school functions, but for local business groups who ask us, other schools, conventions . . . we've also gone on tour. If you or Cindy are interested, watch for tryout dates on the bulletin board outside my door."

"Tryouts? You mean you can't just sign up?"

"Oh no. Only about ten percent of the students who want to join do so. It's a very select group."

Roger considered that statement for a moment. It was apparent that he preferred select groups and considered himself a candidate for any of them, sports related or not. "We'll see," he finally said. There was something hooded and secretive about his expression that Lexi didn't like.

She shook herself free of that thought. She had
no business deciding she didn't like someone without even meeting him first! Besides, it was probably
his size that set Roger apart from most of the others
in the class. She shouldn't be suspicious of him just
because he was three times her size and could snap
her in half like a twig! Lexi made a vow not to let
first impressions color her attitude toward the new
people in school.

The bell interrupted her thoughts. With a determined expression on her face, she headed for
Roger and Cindy.

Todd got there first. He was introducing himself
and welcoming them to Cedar River High when
Lexi stepped up beside him.

"And this is my girlfriend, Lexi Leighton," Todd
continued.

"We're glad you're here," Lexi said graciously.

Roger and Cindy both bobbed their heads as if
they knew that to be true.

Jennifer, Peggy, Anna Marie, Tim, Jerry, Gina,
and Tressa all introduced themselves then. Binky,
whose turn it was to clean the chalkboards, waved
at them with the end of a long eraser. Only Minda
and Egg didn't step forward to greet the newcom-
ers. Minda had gathered her books and hurried out
at the sound of the bell. Egg was busying himself
with a stack of music folders on the floor near Mrs.
Waverly's desk.

"Eggo, come over here!" Todd commanded.
"Don't you want to say hello?"

Doubt flitted across Egg's features, but he
sighed and came forward. "Hi. Welcome to Cedar

River High." He didn't give his name or mention that he and Roger had gone to school together once before.

As Egg turned away, Todd said, "Aren't you going to tell Roger that you guys went to school together once before? I'll bet he doesn't remember it."

Egg's lips tightened and he looked annoyed. With a sigh of resignation, he turned back to the group.

"I'm Edward McNaughton. I think we went to first grade together."

"McNaughton?" Roger's faced screwed up in concentration as he tried to remember. Then he began to chant, "McNaughton, McNuttin, Little Nutty McNothing!" Realization dawned on his features. "Little Nutty McNothing? Is that you?"

He gave a laugh that sent a chill down Lexi's spine. "Sure, I remember you. Skinny little kid with a big nose and a big Adam's apple. You haven't changed a bit!"

Roger turned to his girlfriend. "This was the greatest guy in the world to play jokes on, Cindy. He never caught on. What a laugh."

Then, as if dismissing Egg as nothing more than a minor curiosity from his past, Roger flung a meaty arm around Cindy's shoulders and announced, "We'd better get to our next class. Hope it's better than this one was. That Mrs. Waverly is really a drag."

After the pair had left, Todd and Lexi stared at each other in dismay. In a matter of a few seconds, Roger had managed to belittle both their good friend and their favorite teacher.

"Egg, I'm sorry. . . ." Todd began.

"Forget it," Egg muttered. His cheeks were red as cherries. "Roger Mason hasn't changed at all. He's still a jerk."

The subdued group scattered, leaving Todd and Lexi alone to walk to their next class.

"So that was the famous football hero," Todd muttered. "What did you think?"

"Rude. Inconsiderate. Huge." Lexi ticked off the qualities on her fingertips.

"And his girl?"

"Who could tell? She was stuck to him like Velcro. I don't know if she had a personality of her own or not."

"He'd better be a *really* good athlete," Todd muttered to himself. "Otherwise this isn't going to be worth it."

———

"Are you still studying?" Jennifer's voice sounded panicked over the phone line.

Lexi glanced at Peggy and Binky, who had their books spread out across the Leightons' dining room table.

"Yes. Our report is almost done. I'll put you on speakerphone so everyone can hear you." Lexi punched a button. "I'm so glad I didn't have to work on this group project with Minda. She always puts things off till the last moment."

"Yeah, yeah," Jennifer muttered distractedly. "Tell me about it. Listen, can you guys come over?"

"We still have to type the final draft," Lexi began to protest.

"But you still have a couple days before you need

to turn it in!" Jennifer's voice hung on a wail. "And I need you *now*!"

"What for?" Binky asked.

"Reinforcements. Fresh troops. R and R. Moral support. What more can I tell you?"

"What is it, exactly, that you're doing?" Peggy inquired.

"Baby-sitting. And it's horrible. This kid is totally out of control! I need help."

"I thought you were sitting for a little boy on your block," Lexi said. "Aren't you sitting for someone you know?"

"I thought I knew him or I never would have agreed to this. He looks and acts so sweet when his parents are around that I thought this job would be a breeze. I need money for a sweater I found at the mall, and I thought this would be an easy way to get it." Jennifer gave a sharp laugh. "Hah! There's no sweater in existence worth this kind of hassle."

Suddenly the phone clattered to the floor and Lexi and the others heard Jennifer yell. "No, don't touch that. It might break. . . ."

The sound of shattering glass followed, then Jennifer was back on the line. "Come over here. Now! If any of you are my friends, you will help me in my hour of need. Lexi knows the address." The line went dead.

"She sounded pretty serious," Peggy said with calculated understatement.

"She sounded frantic," Binky corrected. "How old is this kid, anyway? Four? Five?"

"Something like that." Lexi tapped the top of her books with a pencil. "Maybe we could go and give her some moral support and then finish up over there."

"Fine with me," Peggy said with a resigned sigh. "If I ever sound that panicked, I want you to come and bail me out."

They'd packed up their books and gathered their jackets when the doorbell rang.

It was Angela Hardy.

"Hi. I'm bored. Is there anything to do here?" Angela inquired. Angela had come to Cedar River under unusual circumstances. She and her mother had been homeless and had moved into the mission. Now, however, their fortunes had improved, and the sad, frightened girl she'd once been had been replaced by a friendly, confident one.

"Not here, but we're on a rescue mission. Jennifer is trapped with a five-year-old monster. Want to come help free her?" Peggy asked.

"Sounds better than television," Angela agreed. "Let's go."

"I don't see what could be so hard," Binky said as they neared the house. "It's only *one* child, right? What can one little kid do?"

"Whatever it is, he's got Jennifer in a fit." Lexi pushed the doorbell.

There were thumping sounds behind the door for some time before anyone answered. Then the door flew open and a wild-haired, wild-eyed Jennifer stood framed there. Her shirt was untucked from her jeans, her tennis shoes untied, and her ponytail a disheveled mess.

"I thought you'd never get here!" She grabbed Lexi's arm and pulled her inside. The others followed.

The living room they walked into was a mess. Toys were strewn everywhere. Blankets over furniture made make-shift tents around the room. A lamp lay on its side on a glass-topped table. Both lamp and table were cracked and broken.

Jennifer caught the direction of her friends' eyes. "I know, I know. I'll deal with it, but I have to catch him first."

"Where *is* he?" Angela asked, her brown eyes horrified.

"In back. They have a six-foot chain link fence around the whole place. No wonder. It would take a prison to keep this kid in line. Come on, I'll show you."

The backyard was also filled with toys. A swing set, a tree house, big-wheeled trikes, beach balls, tennis racquets, and every other toy imaginable. Careening through it all and screaming at the top of his lungs was a young boy.

"What's the problem?" Lexi had to raise her voice to be heard over the din.

"I said the dreaded word 'bedtime,'" Jennifer yelled back.

"Nooooooo. . . ." The little boy dodged a wagon as he ran. "No bedtime!"

"If one of you guys will run water in the bathtub and another hold the door closed so he can't get away, maybe we can manage this. Angela, you head him off at the pass." Determinedly, Jennifer started after the child. "Ryan, you come here, right now!"

Ryan feinted toward the left but broke right. Angela managed to set herself in his path. He hesitated and Jennifer took advantage of the moment. She scooped him into her arms.

The other girls watched in dumbfounded amazement as Ryan's features convulsed with fury. He began to kick and punch Jennifer with all his might.

Jennifer winced but held on.

"I'm telling my mom on you," Ryan threatened. "She won't pay you and she'll never hire you again."

"Good," Jennifer muttered. "There's not enough money in the world to pay me to do this again anyway."

"I'll say you were mean." His eyes narrowed. It was obvious to see that he was using every trick in his arsenal to manipulate Jennifer into putting him down.

"But you know I'm not," she retorted.

"I'll tell her you hurt me," he threatened.

Jennifer paused. Then she glanced at her friends. "It's a good thing that I have witnesses then, isn't it?"

The little boy frowned. He hadn't thought that one through. Finally he said, "Then I don't want bubbles in my water."

"No bubbles."

"And three stories instead of two."

"Three stories.

"Long ones."

"Okay, long ones."

The bedtime ritual went fairly smoothly from then on.

Exhausted by his physical and emotional antics, Ryan fell asleep two pages into the first story.

Quietly, Jennifer joined her friends on the front porch. She sank into a chair and closed her eyes. "Thanks for coming. I wouldn't have made it without you."

"What do they feed that kid, anyway? Nasty pills?" Binky was indignant. "I've never seen a brattier kid!"

"I'm not quite sure what went wrong," Jennifer said. She wiped a damp sleeve across her forehead. "He was okay until we disagreed on bedtime. Then he went ballistic. It was as though once he got wound up, he *couldn't* calm himself. It was as though he was so emotional he couldn't even *think*."

"I used to know a guy like that," Angela said quietly. She rarely talked about her life before the days at the mission. Everyone gave her their rapt attention.

"He lived in a shelter, like us. No one could say the right thing to him. He was irritable all the time and got mad very easily. Once he got mad, look out. He'd always manage to pick a fight and wouldn't give in, even if he were losing. My mom called him a bully."

"That's a perfect description of Ryan," Jennifer admitted. "If someone doesn't stop him, he's going to bully himself from nursery school right to jail!"

"Are you going to tell his parents?" Peggy asked.

Jennifer shrugged. "Probably not."

"You've *got* to do it!" Binky gasped. "They need to know."

"His parents will only smack him. They're always either spanking him or threatening to do it."

"No wonder he behaves like that! His parents helped to teach him," Binky snorted.

"It's a parent's business about spanking," Jennifer continued, "but it shouldn't be threatened all the time. My dad only spanked me twice—once for running into the street in front of a moving car and once for setting fire to my mom's dining room drapes. I deserved it both times."

"I guess so," Binky muttered.

"But I remember the lesson. Ryan thinks that hitting is the way to solve everything." Jennifer pulled at her blond hair. "What a mess."

"So instead of teaching Ryan to behave, it teaches him to be even more aggressive," Lexi concluded.

"Then what's the right thing to do?" Binky asked.

"My parents still use 'time outs' with Ben," Lexi said. "They never get angry or threaten him, but if he gets too wound up or into trouble for breaking the rules, he has to sit on a chair until he starts to behave. He knows that if he gets upset when he loses a game, he'll end up in the chair, listening to the rest of us play the next one. The rules never vary. Ben has picked it up and he's handicapped. That means there's *no* excuse for a boy like Ryan to behave as he did tonight!"

"But unless Ryan's parents start being decent role models and quit allowing any kind of hitting in the house, he'll never learn how to behave!"

Lexi shuddered. "I hate to think of what kind of boy he'll grow up to be if they don't."

As they spoke, Binky began to frown. With the quick, darting movements she so often used, she started to dig into her backpack.

"What are you looking for?" Peggy asked.

"I have an article in here somewhere that I want to read out loud. It's about bullies." She pawed around in the bag for another moment and then pulled a battered magazine triumphantly out of its depths. "Aha . . . here it is."

She flipped to a premarked page and began to read.

" 'Parents should make sure that their children have the proper social skills. Practice with them if necessary until they know how to handle all situations that might arise. Show children how to get along by having good relationships within your family. Help brothers and sisters to get along. Give your child opportunities to gain self-confidence— classes, groups, and organizations such as—' "

"What have you got this stuff for?" Jennifer interrupted. "Are you doing a report for school?"

Binky began to blush. It began at the base of her neck and reddened her cheeks, forehead, and even her ears. She looked like she'd been set on fire.

"Bink? You don't have to be embarrassed. We do reports all the time."

"It's not that."

"What'd you do, 'borrow' the magazine from the library without checking it out?" Jennifer asked warily.

"Of course not!" Binky was indignant. "I don't do things like that."

"Then what?"

"I just happened to get the article for Egg, that's all."

"And you're embarrassed by that?" Jennifer was growing more and more puzzled. "Why? Because Egg can't do his own research?"

Binky gave a huge sigh. "Egg doesn't know about it yet. I'm taking it home to him because I want him to read it. He needs to know something more about bullies, that's all. There wasn't much available on the subject, so I took everything I could get. Even the stuff for parents about little kids."

"You're going to have to clear this up for me," Angela said. "Why do you want Egg to read about bullies?"

"Because Roger Mason is really getting to him," Binky blurted. "There, now you know. And you have to promise never to mention to Egg that I told you."

"What do you mean, 'getting to him'?" Peggy asked.

"Making him nervous. Egg's got a lot of bad memories about Roger. He wasn't just a little bit mean to my brother. He was horrible. And Egg doesn't think Roger's grown out of it. He might be bigger, but otherwise he hasn't changed a bit."

"How can Egg even say that?" Jennifer protested. "Has he actually talked to Roger?"

"Not much."

"Has he had anything to do with him?"

"Not really."

"Then Egg is being silly," Angela concluded. "I agree with Jennifer. I think Egg worries too much."

Binky turned to Lexi with pleading eyes.

"Sorry, Bink, but this time I kind of agree with the others. What Roger and Egg experienced was a long time ago. I can't believe that both guys haven't grown up."

"Egg's being silly," Peggy assured Binky. "You know he worries about everything. Frankly, I can't figure out how he can still be bothered by something that happened that long ago."

Binky sighed and shook her head. She didn't argue. All she said was, "Just wait and see."

Chapter Four

Lexi shifted her school books on her hip as she grasped the doorknob on the front door. She had homework in every class tonight and she wasn't happy about it. She'd hoped to visit her grandmother at the nursing home, but now that would have to wait. Unusual sounds inside the house beckoned her within. With dismay, she realized the sounds she heard were that of her little brother, Benjamin, crying.

She dropped her books on a table by the door and hurried into the living room where Ben lay sprawled across the couch, sobbing as though his heart were breaking. Her mother stood over him, rubbing his back and murmuring soothing sounds, but her expression was tense and angry.

"Mom? Ben?"

Ben turned a bright red, tear-stained face to his sister and began to cry, if it were possible, even harder.

"What's happened?" Lexi felt panic rise within her. "Is he hurt? Do we need a doctor?"

Mrs. Leighton shook her head and signaled for Lexi to be quiet. As she did so, Ben's cries began to taper off into whimpers, then the whimper to a whine. Finally the whine turned to an exhausted snore. He'd cried himself to sleep.

Lexi handed her mother a soft, downy blanket, and Mrs. Leighton covered her son. Together, mother and daughter tiptoed into the kitchen.

"What's going on?" Lexi demanded. She pulled a pitcher of juice from the fridge and poured herself a glass. "I've never seen him cry so hard—even the times he's gotten lost."

"Those boys were picking on Thomas and Ben again. Thomas had come over after school and they were building a racetrack for their little cars in the sandbox. I've been baking all day, so I was watching them from the kitchen window. Then the nursing home called to let me know that your grandmother needed to have her medication changed. I got caught on hold while calling the doctor and by the time I got back to the window, Thomas had run home and those awful boys were terrorizing Ben."

"I wish I'd come home sooner," Lexi muttered. "If I'd caught those boys . . ."

"Violence for violence doesn't help anything, honey. You know that."

"I know. Proverbs 15:1," Lexi quoted. " 'A gentle answer turns away wrath, but a harsh word stirs up anger.' I realize that, Mom, but this makes me so *mad*."

Mrs. Leighton smiled. "Then how about 'Do not be quickly provoked in your spirit, for anger resides in the lap of fools'?"

"There's a verse for everything, isn't there?"

"Seems to be." Mrs. Leighton ruffled her fingers through her daughter's hair. "And I think I looked all the anger verses up in the Bible while I was trying to calm down. Seeing Ben so hurt made my blood boil."

A noise in the living room alerted them that Ben was awake. They entered to see him sitting on the couch holding the blanket, a thumb in his mouth.

That thumb was a sure sign that Ben was still agitated. He hadn't sucked his thumb for a long time, and when he did, it was always to calm himself after an upset.

"Thirsty?" Mrs. Leighton asked. "I always am after a cry."

Ben nodded. At the table, his mother put a big glass of juice in front of him which he slurped down with amazing speed.

"Want to play a game or work on a puzzle?" Lexi asked, hoping to distract him from troubling thoughts. Ben was deeply sensitive and attuned to others' feelings and needs. To be hurt this way, by his peers, was no doubt devastating to Ben.

"Puzzle."

Lexi took a simple, brightly colored puzzle from the stack inside a nearby cupboard and put it on the table. Ben tipped it over to dismantle it. Then, one by one, they took turns putting it back together.

Just as Ben was about to put the tail back on a roaring lion, he looked up at Lexi and asked, "Why?"

"Why are you putting the tail on the lion? Because that's the last piece, silly!"

"No, Lexi. Why do those boys pick on me? Why do they make me cry? I never did anything to them."

"Oh, Ben. . . ." Lexi's heart felt as though it were tearing in her chest.

"I wanna be friends with them. Don't they know that?" Ben's hurt and confusion showed in his eyes.

"They just aren't very nice boys, Ben. They like to pick on kids weaker or littler than themselves, like you and Thomas, to make themselves feel big and tough."

"I could be tough. See?" Ben curled a scrawny arm to make a muscle. "Would they like me if I were tough like them?" He got up from the table and began to chant. "Dumbbells. Babies. Stupid little babies."

"Ben, don't. . . ." Lexi tried to stop her brother, but he continued.

"I be mean too." Ben swung fists in the air as though he were hitting an invisible opponent. He stopped when he saw his mother standing in the doorway, hands on her hips, and a pained expression on her face.

"Come here, sweetie," she said softly as she sat down on a chair and invited Ben into her lap. He was getting tall, all arms and legs, but he eagerly climbed up and curled in close to his mother.

"We don't want you to be mean, Ben. Then you'd be acting as badly as those boys."

"But I'd be *brave*."

Ben's chin began to tremble and he didn't look brave at all.

"You are afraid of those boys, aren't you?" His mother scraped dark hair from his eyes as he nodded.

"That's okay. I'd be scared too if someone bigger and older decided to pick on me. Everyone is afraid of being bullied. Even the boys who pick on you are afraid of being bullied by someone bigger and stronger than themselves. That's part of why they choose to pick on you. They want to feel strong and in control. They think that by using nasty words and even physical violence they'll appear tougher. They're afraid of looking soft and weak."

Though Ben obviously didn't understand everything his mother was saying, he seemed to be picking up the gist of her words.

"There are people who, all their lives, try to boss everyone they know—their wives, their children, their employees. These people think that if they don't act tough, no one will respect them. They are afraid to show their feelings."

"Like being scared?" Ben asked.

"Exactly."

"Like crying?" He wiped an errant tear from his own eye.

"Yes. Sometimes we adults don't think about what we're doing and we'll say to someone like you, 'Big boys don't cry.'"

"I'm a big boy."

"Yes you are. But that doesn't mean that it's not okay to cry once in a while." Mrs. Leighton smiled gently at Ben. "Do you understand?"

"Sissies cry."

"No, that's not always true. Sometimes the bravest thing a person can do is to admit his real feelings to others. It's very hard to admit weakness. The boys who tease you want to look tough. Instead, to me, they seem weak and cowardly."

"And naughty," Ben concluded. He knew what that word meant.

A noise outside caught his attention. "Wiggles!" He squirmed off his mother's lap. "I gotta go play with Wiggles and feed my bunny."

"You do that," Mrs. Leighton agreed with a smile. "I'm sure bunny is hungry."

After Ben had disappeared through the door, Mrs. Leighton slumped in her chair and put her head in her hands. "Do you think he understood what I was trying to say?"

"Some of it," Lexi responded. "And he knows you love and accept him just the way he is. It doesn't get much better than that. . . . Mom, are *you* crying?"

Mrs. Leighton angrily scrubbed away a tear that had escaped down her cheek.

"Out of anger and frustration, Lexi. I am so furious with those boys and what they've done to Ben and Thomas that I could just scream!"

"That would be productive," Lexi said with a gentle note of sarcasm.

"I just have to get my thoughts together and decide what I'm going to do. I can't let this go on. Thomas's mother says he's *afraid* to go to school now. Those children have to be stopped."

"Bullies aren't very smart if you ask me. All the other kids must really dislike them. It's really much easier to have friends than to have enemies."

Mrs. Leighton nodded. Already her mind was beginning to churn. Lexi recognized the signs. Her mother wouldn't rest until she had an idea for dealing with this situation.

Twenty minutes later, after Lexi had started her homework, Mrs. Leighton came back into the kitchen and announced, "I've got it!"

She sat down at the table, across from Lexi. "I'm going to visit the next school board meeting and request that they implement an all-out campaign against bullying. It needs to begin in kindergarten and be followed through all the way to senior high. Children need to know that this type of behavior is totally unacceptable. This is not something that just parents have to enforce. Teachers are with children seven or eight hours a day. We all need to work together."

"Is that really necessary?" Lexi asked doubtfully. "For a few mean boys? Couldn't they just be punished? Wouldn't that be easier?"

"Easier, but not more effective." Mrs. Leighton waved the women's magazine she'd been carrying. "I picked this up to read for a few minutes just to relax, and what did I find? An entire article on this behavior in children! According to the author, bullying is a serious problem that has to be nipped in the bud. It recommends that parents and schools work together on the issue."

"But, Mom, maybe Ben isn't able to defend himself—or Thomas either—but most kids should be able to handle a bully, shouldn't they? I had a really rotten time when we moved to Cedar River and Minda Hannaford and the High Fives tried to make me do things I didn't want to do. Still, I finally figured out how to handle her. Isn't that something kids just need to learn?"

"Like the saying 'Boys will be boys'? I don't think so. You believe I'm getting overly upset because Ben was involved but . . ."

"Involved in what?" Dr. Leighton stood in the doorway with a frown on his face. He'd just come from his veterinary clinic. He was wearing heavy jeans and a sweat shirt. That meant he'd been called to one of the stables to work on horses.

"Hi, Dad." Lexi looked to her mother to fill him in on what had been going on today.

When Mrs. Leighton was done, Dr. Leighton sank into a chair. His expression was sober.

"Do *you* think I'm making too much of this, Jim?" Mrs. Leighton asked. "Do you think Lexi is right—that kids just have to work these things out for themselves?"

When he remained silent, his wife continued. "It hurts my heart to see vulnerable kids like Ben and Thomas suffer. There's no way they have the skills to defend themselves against a bully. Thomas's parents moved to a new neighborhood to give him a fresh start, and this is happening already! Some kids will always be victims and others will always be cruel unless they are taught bullying is inappropriate and will be punished—by everyone—not just parents."

"I don't know how you'd enforce it, Mom. Lots of junk goes on at school that the teachers never see."

"But we have to *try*. Don't we?"

Dr. Leighton frowned. "I think you are both right. It's a nearly impossible situation to correct, and yet something has to be done about it. I've often wondered if my life in school might have been different if someone had taken Marilyn's attitude and tried to do something constructive about the issue."

"Your life?" Lexi's amazement was undeniable.

"Don't sound so surprised. I was a skinny little kid once too, you know. As I've told you before, a boy in my class decided that I was the one person he should pick on. I was told by my parents not to fight, so he knew I wouldn't hurt him like the other boys might. He used to knock books out of my hands, steal my lunch, trip me when I went to the black-board. . . ."

"Why do kids do it, Dad?"

Dr. Leighton gave a wry smile. "Because it works. After all, if he stole my lunch, he got *two* for himself. If he shoved me off my bike, then he got to ride. It's a way to get what you want. What's more, it had to give him a feeling of control, of power over me. Men have fought wars over power, Lexi. It's not so surprising that little boys like the feeling of it as well."

He gave a sigh. "Unfortunately, like in war, there's always an innocent victim, somebody who gets hurt."

"Like you? Like Thomas and Ben?"

Dr. Leighton nodded. "Exactly like us."

"You sound as if this happened *yesterday*, Jim."

"In some ways it feels like yesterday. Kids do grow up, but they don't always forget the hurt."

"Have you noticed the weird friendship of the week?" Jennifer inquired snidely as she met Lexi at their lockers. Her eyes were on a couple at the end of the hall.

Lexi glanced in the direction Jennifer was staring.

"Tim and Matt? That's not so odd."

"Not them. *Them!*" Jennifer pointed with the book she held in her hand.

Cindy Jarvis and Anna Marie Arnold were deep in conversation, standing so close to each other that their heads nearly touched. Cindy was gesturing and Anna Marie was nodding eagerly.

"What's up with them?" Jennifer inquired. "I thought Cindy and Roger would have to be surgically separated to get them apart, and then, in the last couple days, she seems to have latched on to Anna Marie when Roger's not around."

"Just being friendly, probably," Lexi said, not quite believing it even as she spoke.

"Yeah, right. Friendly? Miss I-Don't-Even-Know-You-Peons-Exist Jarvis? Get real!"

"Okay, so that doesn't sound very plausible. It still could be true. It must get pretty boring for Cindy, spending all her time with Roger."

"I'm sure it is," Jennifer muttered. "And a real bummer too. I'll bet they fight about who gets to stand in front of the mirror."

"Oh, don't be such a grouch. Just because you took an instinctive dislike to them doesn't mean they aren't nice people."

"Mark my words, Lexi. You'll see it for yourself soon." Jennifer slammed her locker door shut. "I just hate to see poor, innocent Anna Marie get sucked up by that . . . vampire."

Though she wouldn't admit it to Jennifer, that had been worrying Lexi too. Anna Marie was a shy girl with soft brown curls and pale blue eyes. When Lexi had first met her, Anna Marie was overweight and extremely self-conscious about her size. Anna Marie's nickname had been "Banana Anna" because of her love for banana splits. Then she'd begun to diet and carried that to the other extreme and become anorexic. Her compulsive personality didn't seem to allow her to do anything halfway. Now, after treatment, she was a normal weight and size and finally coming out of her shell. Still, she seemed vulnerable. Was she able to handle someone with as forceful a personality as Cindy?

"Where'd you drift off to?" Jennifer inquired, snapping Lexi back to the present.

"Just thinking about what you said."

"Rumor has it that Cindy has 'decided' that Anna Marie is going to be her new best friend. I wonder if Anna Marie had any say in the matter."

"She looks happy enough," Lexi pointed out. The two girls were still whispering and laughing together. Several students had walked by the pair and said hello, but Lexi noticed that neither girl responded.

"Looks to me like Cindy's starting some exclusive little club for herself and Anna Marie." Jennifer snorted. "That's something. The High Fives aren't good enough for her! I wonder how they like that."

"Aren't you being just a little harsh?" Lexi asked. "Maybe you're imagining everything."

"Look at Anna Marie and tell me what I'm 'imagining.'"

Jennifer was right. Anna Marie's features beamed from the attention she was receiving from Cindy, but there was a look of puzzlement, of questioning, in her face as well. It was a "why me?" sort of look that spoke volumes.

"We both know how quiet Anna Marie is," Jennifer continued. "She's not accustomed to quite so much attention. Something's going on and I'm going to find out what it is."

At that moment, Cindy left Anna Marie and turned down another hall. Anna Marie walked slowly toward Jennifer and Lexi.

"Hi," Jennifer said brightly. "You're just the person I wanted to see."

"I am?" There was surprise in Anna Marie's voice.

"Sure. I'm going to have a sleepover at my house this weekend." Lexi's eyebrows rose as Jennifer spoke. This was the first she'd heard of a sleepover. "I'm asking Lexi, Binky, Peggy, and Angela. Can you come?"

Anna Marie's face lit with pleasure. "Sure. I'd love to." She looked at her watch. "Gotta go. See you later."

"Well, Sherlock Holmes," Lexi said after Anna Marie left. "I suppose this is your idea of an investigation."

"Elementary, my dear Lexi. Elementary." With a waggle of her eyebrows, Jennifer started down the hall.

"Hi, Mom. Can Jennifer and I make cookies? We've had the need for chocolate all day long. Maybe chocolatey chocolate chip cookies. . . ."

"With chocolate frosting," Jennifer added.

"And we'll eat them with chocolate milk!" the girls chimed together and began to laugh until they realized that Mrs. Leighton was not laughing with them.

"Mom? Are you okay?" Lexi went to the sink where her mother was standing with a glass in her hands. They were shaking.

Episodes such as this were not uncommon with Mrs. Leighton's multiple sclerosis. But the look on her mom's face told Lexi it was something more.

"Just angry and frustrated, honey." Mrs. Leighton held out her hands. "Look at me. I got so upset this afternoon that I started to tremble all over. Can you believe it? Even my MS doesn't make me do that!"

"Did you hit a snag in your bullying campaign?" Lexi asked sympathetically. Ever since the last incident with Ben and Thomas, her mother had been like a whirlwind, reading articles, composing letters, and writing notes on what she wanted to say to school administration.

"Snag? Roadblock is more like it. Actually, what I hit felt like a *mountain*. An immovable, impossible mountain."

"So what was it?" Jennifer asked. She was familiar with what Lexi's mother was doing.

"I had an appointment with the principals of two elementary schools today, and frankly, the response I received *shocked* me. I was so well prepared with documentation and proposals for change that I felt sure they'd have to listen to me."

"And?"

"I was met with complete indifference! Do you know what they told me? 'Boys will be boys, Mrs. Leighton. We are very sorry about your handicapped son and his little friend, but I think you might have more luck protecting them until they learn to handle the problem.' Oh!" Mrs. Leighton sank onto a kitchen stool. "I was so infuriated and offended that I nearly cried."

"Some good that would have done," she muttered to herself. "Then they would have told me *I* was the problem because I couldn't handle bullies either!"

"So no one thinks this is important?" Jennifer asked.

"Apparently not. At least not the people I talked to today." That comment seemed to give Mrs. Leighton an idea. "So I'll have to talk to other people. People who have to listen."

She jumped to her feet and ran her fingers through her hair. "I'll go to the school board. They have to listen to me. It's a public forum." She frowned. "But I can't go until I'm completely prepared. Lexi, will you cook supper? I have to go to the library and do some more research."

"But Mom . . . ."

"There are pork chops to fry and potatoes already in the oven. Ben is playing with Thomas. I'll try to be back, but if I'm not, don't worry about me. I plan to stay there until I get enough information to argue my case." Mrs. Leighton grabbed the keys for the car and went out the door.

"Wow," Jennifer said after Mrs. Leighton was gone. "She's really enthusiastic."

"I know." Lexi sighed. "I wish she'd stick to painting. I'm not sure either that there's much to be done about bullies. Maybe Mom is fighting a losing battle."

"I doubt it," Jennifer said sagely. "If she's anything like my mother, she'll do everything she can to make sure her kids are safe. Like my dad says, 'Never underestimate the power of a mother.'"

"Maybe you're right. Come on, let's make those cookies."

———

Lexi was placing a platter of pork chops on the

table when her mother returned. Ben and Dr. Leighton were already at the table.

"Lexi, you are a doll. Supper looks lovely." Mrs. Leighton's eyes were bright with excitement.

"Did you have a good trip to the library?" Jim Leighton asked.

"Yes. It was extremely interesting." Mrs. Leighton darted a glance at Ben, who after table grace had dug into his dinner with gusto. "I'll tell you all about it later."

Lexi could tell that her mother was eager to share what she'd learned and more than a little impatient for Ben to go to bed.

Mrs. Leighton hurried him through his bath and bedtime stories and had him tucked in fifteen minutes early. Then, with a stack of books on her arm, she came into the family room where Lexi and Mr. Leighton were seated.

"Just wait till you hear this," she began.

"I take it that you didn't want Ben to hear what you've learned," Dr. Leighton said with a smile.

"Not really. Ben doesn't need to hear about unpleasantness that he can't do anything about. I think the information might upset him. Did you know that many suicides are attributed to bullying?"

That caught Lexi's attention. Peggy's boyfriend Chad had committed suicide, and it had been devastating to the entire gang.

"It's true. I read the newspaper articles. Students—mostly boys—have killed themselves to avoid harsh bullying by classmates. And gangs are nothing more than groups of bullies relying on the fact that people are too frightened to tell on them.

For a fee, they'll agree not to hurt a business or a person. They scare people into not telling anyone what's going on."

"Are you sure?" Lexi asked. "Isn't this kind of farfetched?"

"Not at all. We don't take bullying seriously, but we should—especially school personnel because most bullying occurs in schools.

"Until recently, I was as guilty as the next person," Mrs. Leighton admitted ruefully, "because I, too, thought bullying was just one of those things kids faced in childhood and then eventually outgrew."

"And isn't it usually?" Lexi asked.

"That means we assume that every child can take care of himself or herself, stand up for his rights or refuse to be pushed around. What's more, we assume that if children *can't* defend themselves, then they deserve whatever they get. We know that Ben and Thomas can't defend themselves—and I hardly think you believe either boy deserves the treatment they've been getting."

"When you put it that way . . ." Lexi frowned. She'd known lots of bullies. It had been hard to stand up to the High Fives but she'd done it. But there was no way Ben could have done the same thing. A child with Down's syndrome was at a complete disadvantage and virtually helpless to handle a bully.

"Listen to this." Mrs. Leighton spread photocopied papers across the table. "According to my research, the vast majority of children are not bullies or the victims of bullies. Most children, properly raised, develop innate restraints against that kind of behavior. But the percent who become bullies do so at a very early age."

"Then they must *like* being bullies," Lexi concluded.

"I'm not so sure about that. They may not know anything different. Also their behavior interferes with making true friends and having good mental health."

"It also interferes with school," Lexi added. "People who spend too much time picking on other people don't get their own stuff done—like homework."

"The saddest thing I discovered was that bullies don't change once they're grown up. Bullies are more likely to abuse their wives, commit crimes—and raise more bullies."

"Terrific," Lexi groaned. "Someday Minda will have little Minda-bullies!"

"Can girls bully like boys?" Dr. Leighton asked. "I always think of guys as being the bullying kind."

"Of course they can. While boys are more physical and aggressive, girls can be subtle and mean."

"Sneaky," Lexi supplied. "That's what girls can be."

"So you *do* understand!" Mrs. Leighton's cheeks were flushed. She leaned back in her chair with a satisfied sigh.

"Marilyn," Jim began. "We understand how important this is to you, but don't you think you might want to take it a little bit easier? Is all this emotional excitement good for your health?"

Mrs. Leighton waved away the suggestion with a dismissing movement of her hand. "Nonsense. Having Ben suffer is what makes me ill. Doing something productive can only help."

Chapter Five

"What a wimp!"

The harsh words were followed by uncomfortable laughter.

"Butter fingers! Can't you do *anything* right?"

"What's going on in the music room?" Todd asked Lexi.

"Who knows? I'm not sure I want to find out."

Ignoring her statement, he turned into the room, dragging Lexi with him. The scene before them spoke for itself.

Egg, who had been designated by Mrs. Waverly to sort, stack, and put away the mounds of sheet music used that day, stood in the middle of a semicircle of students. The music lay spread out around him in a disorderly clutter. It would take at least a half hour to re-sort the pages, making sure each was in the right folder again. Egg's face and neck were a painful red and his eyes were cast downward.

"What a klutz," Roger said scornfully. "You haven't changed a bit since we were in grade school together." Then, dismissing Egg as though he were a mosquito on his jacket, he turned to the other guys. "Let's go shoot a few hoops."

The others, without a backward glance, trooped after Roger.

Egg remained frozen to the spot.

"What happened?" Todd asked softly as he knelt to the floor and began to pick up the scattered pages.

"I'll do it. Just leave it." Egg's voice was harsh and raspy, roughened by unshed tears.

"Don't be silly." Lexi knelt beside Todd. "Working together, we can have this done in just a few minutes."

"I said *leave it*."

Todd stood up and took Egg by the arm. "Listen to me, Egg, and listen good. Don't let that guy get to you. He's a jerk. Anybody who enjoys someone else's discomfort is a piece of trash. I know you're frustrated, but don't take it out on the people who want to help you. Got that?"

Not waiting for a response, Todd bent to pick up more of the music. Silently, Egg followed.

By the time Binky found them, the music was back in its proper files. Lexi and Todd were talking with unusual animation. Egg was quiet.

"I told the others we'd meet them at the Hamburger Shack," Binky said. "Egg, are you just finishing that music now? Hurry up or we'll be late."

"I'm not going." Egg shut the door of the music file with a slam.

Binky's eyes grew wide. "What's bugging you?"

"Nothing. I'm just not going, okay? Do you get that?"

Binky looked to Lexi and Todd for an explanation.

Todd took Egg by the arm and led him to the door. "Let's just get into my car. We can talk about this there."

"What? Talk about what?" Binky trotted along with questions all the way to the parking lot.

Once inside the car, Todd spoke. "Roger was harassing Egg today. Egg accidentally dropped the music files and Roger was giving Egg a hard time about it. He made some jokes."

"And everyone else laughed," Egg added forlornly.

"They didn't know what else to do, Egg," Lexi pointed out logically. "That's a pretty awkward position to be in, you know."

"Then how come everybody followed him out to shoot hoops? And how come nobody defended me?" The hurt in Egg's voice was painful to hear.

No one had an answer for that. They sat quietly, listening to the wind whistle through a partially cracked window in the car. Finally Egg spoke.

"I didn't drop those papers."

"Then how did they get on the floor?" Binky asked.

"I mean, I didn't drop them by accident. Roger tripped me."

Lexi and Todd looked horrified. "Why didn't you say something?"

"Or make him help you clean up?"

Egg's laugh was dry and humorless. "Yeah, right. Like that would have worked. He would have denied it. That's probably what he *wanted* me to do!"

A loud *thunk* reverberated in the back as Binky punched her fist into a stack of school books. "Owwww!"

"What'd you do *that* for?" Egg muttered.

"Because I'm so mad I could spit, that's why," Binky fumed like a little volcano. "What's wrong with those people, anyway? Aren't they *human*?"

"Roger and who else?" Todd inquired mildly.

"His girlfriend, Cindy, of course."

"Cindy wasn't in the music room," Lexi pointed out.

"That doesn't mean she wasn't out and about causing trouble."

"Has she been bugging you?" Egg asked, his frown so deep his eyebrows met in the middle of his forehead.

"Understatement of the week," Binky growled. "She's been driving me *nuts*. Hasn't anyone else noticed?"

Todd and Lexi glanced at each other and shrugged. "Not really."

"See? That just proves how *sneaky* she is. Anna Marie hasn't spoken to me all week and I know that's Cindy's doing."

"What does Anna Marie have to do with any of this?" Todd was puzzled.

"Cindy's 'adopted' Anna Marie. She's Cindy's new best friend. I suppose Cindy needed something to do while Roger was at practice." Binky looked at Todd pityingly. "You don't have a clue how girls like that work, do you?"

"Girls like who? Work how?" Todd looked helplessly to Lexi for an explanation.

Binky didn't give her time to explain. "Sneaky," she volunteered. "Behind people's backs. Threats and warnings. Saying things like, 'If you talk to Binky, I'll never talk to you again.'"

"Girls actually *do* that?" Todd sounded horrified. "That's really petty."

"I'm afraid Binky is right," Lexi affirmed. "Girls

can be bullies too. They are as good as guys at intimidating others. Why are you surprised? You've known Minda and the High Fives a long time."

Todd digested that bit of information. "I suppose so, now that I think about it. I guess I just assumed that all bullies were guys."

Binky snorted in an unladylike fashion. "That shows how little you know! We girls suffer too. I'm sure poor Anna Marie doesn't know what's hit her."

"Girls are much more verbal than guys," Lexi explained. "They use threats and taunts. I remember a girl who, in fourth grade, managed to exclude me from all the games on the playground. She called me names and spread rumors about me."

"What did you do?" Binky asked.

"Nothing. She moved after only three months in our school and everything went back to normal. I guess you and Egg can't hope to be that lucky."

"It looks as though this is 'Get the McNaughtons' week," Binky said in resignation. "Maybe Cindy and Roger will lose interest in us soon."

"Don't count on it," Egg muttered grimly.

———

The entire gang minus Anna Marie met at the Hamburger Shack. Jennifer, who was the last to arrive, came waving a newspaper.

"What's this?" Peggy pulled at the corner of the paper.

"There's a big write-up in the sports section about Roger and how he's going to save our school's sports record from 'another unremarkable year.'"

"That says a lot for the rest of us," Todd said with a frown. "Pretty uncomplimentary for all of us who've been working hard here for more than a few days."

"Roger is quoted as saying, 'I don't think it's too late. I believe I can still turn this team around,' " Jennifer read. Then she grinned nastily. "Aren't you glad he came?"

The boys all protested loudly. Ignoring them, Jennifer continued reading.

" 'Mason has big potential,' says Coach Drummond, 'and the strength to really help the team. He is a big asset to our football program.' "

"No wonder he thinks he's so smart," Binky grumbled. "Everybody tells him he is!"

"Look at that." Matt, who had been silent, pointed toward the door.

Roger and two other guys had entered. All three swaggered to the counter as if they were superheroes on the way to some big mission. Behind them were three little boys staring up at the older ones in awe. All three children were trying to imitate the cocky, swaying walk. From where they were sitting, Todd, Lexi, and the others could hear the boys.

"Roger, Roger, we got a ball. You want to throw a few with us?"

"Nah. I'm busy. Thanks anyway." Roger's lip curled as he turned away from the children.

"Maybe later?" one boy asked hopefully.

"Maybe."

"Could we get your autograph?" A little fellow with a shock of red hair and a heavy sprinkle of freckles held up a tattered piece of notebook paper.

Roger rolled his eyes, but when he turned to the kids, he wore a big grin. "Why not? What are you going to do with it? Sell it for big money?"

"I'm gonna frame mine!" Freckle-face said as he watched Roger scrawl something on the paper using his leg for a table.

When all three slips of paper had been signed and effusive thanks given, the children backed out the door of the Hamburger Shack waving and grinning.

Roger and his buddies burst into peals of scornful laughter.

"Little nerds," Roger hooted.

"You really had them going! They're going to *frame* your autograph!"

Lexi was relieved to see that Roger and friends had ordered food to go and left as soon as it was ready. She was beginning to feel uncomfortable being in the same room with him.

When the door closed behind them, Egg gave a growl of frustration. "Did you see that? Those little boys think Roger Mason is the greatest invention since the computer, and he just laughs at them behind their backs. This hero worship of that guy really makes me mad."

"At least he didn't laugh in their faces," Peggy pointed out.

"Not this time, but I wouldn't put it past him." Egg's face was growing red. "Roger is no hero. Just the opposite. Why is everybody being fooled?"

"Egg, you had a head start. You knew Roger before. It will take some time for him to show his true colors to everyone else," Todd pointed out.

"Or maybe most people will never know," Lexi added. "You are Roger's chosen 'victim.' Maybe he won't try it with anyone else."

Egg frowned. "He doesn't have that much self-control. I'm sure of it. One day he'll cross somebody who won't stand for it."

The group was silent. The unspoken question running through their minds was, *Why couldn't Egg be the one who wouldn't put up with Roger's bad behavior?*

The misery on Egg's face told at least part of the answer. He didn't dare. And he didn't know how.

"Keep your feet in the water!" Peggy ordered as Jennifer tried to lift her toes out of the pan of warm, bubble-filled liquid her feet were soaking in.

"This is too weird for me. Besides, my feet are ticklish. I don't think I want a pedicure."

"Of course you do. It's 'the ultimate in luxury,' my new magazine says. Aren't you relaxed yet?"

"Hardly. Can't I have a manicure instead? I like having my fingernails done."

"No. We've come this far. I want to try it." Peggy frowned. "Do you have any old rose petals lying around? The magazine says that rose petals in the water make a nice fragrance."

"Funny, but I just ran out of rose petals yesterday," Jennifer joked. "I'll have to have my handsome prince send me some more."

The slumber party at Jennifer's was in full swing. Beauty makeovers were happening everywhere.

Binky came out of the bathroom holding a tube. "Does anyone know how much of this beauty mask I'm supposed to put on? Has anyone tried it before?"

"I just bought it at the dollar store," Jennifer said. "It was in the super sale basket. Read the directions."

" 'Cover your face in soothing green gel, sit back,

and let the organic nutrients work their magic on your skin,' " Binky read.

"So do it. Owww!" Angela gave a yelp of pain. "It feels like you're plucking out my brains!"

"Not unless your brains are attached to your eyebrows," Lexi said calmly. "Now hold still."

"Okay, if you think this will work. . . ." Binky made her way back into the bathroom.

"That tickles!" Jennifer squealed as Peggy attempted to dry her toes in the towel she'd spread across her lap.

"Think about something else," Peggy ordered. "Tonight is supposed to be a pampering session, and I'm going to pamper you even if it hurts."

Jennifer grimaced and closed her eyes as if trying to conjure up a thought that would distract her from whatever Peggy was trying to do to her feet. When she looked down, Peggy had stuffed little wads of cotton between each toe.

"What's that for?"

"Never mind. Think about something else." Peggy worked determinedly, consulting the magazine for its step-by-step instructions for foot beauty.

"Okay. Why isn't Anna Marie here yet? Then *she* could be having a pedicure instead of me."

Lexi and Angela both looked up, startled, as if they hadn't yet realized their friend was missing.

"She *said* she'd be here," Jennifer whined. "She promised."

"Actually, it's pretty strange that she hasn't come yet," Lexi commented. "She was really excited about this evening. She said she hadn't seen enough of us lately and was looking forward to the night."

"Then maybe she's just late," Peggy offered.

"It's after ten. She'd never be that late."

The girls were quiet for a while, considering where Anna Marie might be. Then a piercing scream split the air.

Binky staggered into the room from the bathroom. Her face was covered with a sickening green paste mask. The goop was a quarter-inch thick and covered all but Binky's eyes, nostrils, and a tiny crack around her mouth.

"Hup mo," the mouth muttered.

"Huh?" Jennifer peered into the frantic eyes behind the mask. "I can't understand you."

"Hup mo!" The unintelligible words sounded panicked. Binky was dancing on her tiptoes and pointing at her face.

"Wash that stuff off so we can understand you," Jennifer ordered.

Binky danced harder. "Uh caaat!"

"She said, 'I can't!'" Lexi translated. "And before that, I think she said, 'Help me.' Binky, can you get this stuff off your face?"

Binky's head flew from side to side in a forceful "no."

Jennifer pulled her feet off Peggy's lap and headed for the bathroom. She returned with the tube of facial mask. "How long did you leave it on? It says to wash it off in ten minutes."

Binky held her fingers in the air to indicate that she'd left it on twenty-five minutes.

Jennifer tapped at the mask with her fingernail. "It's rock hard. I worked with clay once in art class. It dried just like that."

"Hup mo!" Binky clawed at her face, trying to chip away the green muck.

"It also says, 'Do not use after expiration date,' " Lexi read from the tube she'd taken from Jennifer. She gasped. "Binky, this stuff expired almost a *year* ago!"

The scream that emanated from the hideous mask would have scared the bravest of men.

"We've got to get it off her," Lexi said.

"I'm never buying from the super sale bin at the dollar store again," Jennifer muttered.

"How much did you pay for it?" Peggy asked.

Only Binky seemed panicked by the problem of the moment.

"A dime."

"No wonder. For a dime . . ."

"Hup mo!"

"All right, all right. What should we try first?"

Peggy picked at the hardening facial mask. "It doesn't want to peel off. Do the directions say we should soak it off?"

"The directions probably expired with the glop inside," Angela said bluntly.

"But we have to try something." Peggy took charge. "Binky, lie down. Lexi, get some warm, wet towels. Jennifer, you find a knife."

At that, Binky began to squeal and jump up and down.

"Okay, a spoon, then. Anything to scrape this stuff off her face."

The girls hovered over Binky, prone on the bed, taking turns running for more warm, wet towels and chipping away at the green mess that was quickly turning into something similar to plaster of paris. They worked for nearly half an hour before Jennifer stood back and announced, "There! I think we got it."

Binky leaped to her feet and headed for the mirror. "My face—you ruined it!"

"It's just a little red from all the rubbing," Lexi said calmly. "It'll be fine tomorrow."

"I look like I have a sunburn," Binky wailed.

"Better that than a permanent mask," Angela pointed out.

"I think your skin looks 'fresh and new,' just like it says on the tube," Jennifer added.

The phone rang then, saving Jennifer from Binky's fury.

"Hello, Goldens' residence," Jennifer said into the receiver. "Anna Marie! We were wondering what happened to you. Are you coming?"

The others grew quiet, waiting.

"You aren't? Why? Are you okay? You sound funny." Jennifer frowned as she spoke. Impatiently she added, "Come on, Anna Marie, we've been friends a long time. You can tell me the truth."

After a few moments, Jennifer hung up the phone.

"Well," Binky demanded. "What did she say?"

"She's not coming."

"We figured that much out," Peggy said impatiently. "Why?"

"She wasn't going to tell me, but she finally admitted it was because of Cindy."

"What does she have to do with our slumber party?" Angela asked.

"She told Anna Marie not to come." Jennifer plopped herself down on the edge of the bed. She looked upset. "Cindy has picked Anna Marie to be her best friend, and Cindy wants the relationship to be exclusive. Cindy wants total loyalty and doesn't want Anna Marie hanging around with us."

"Or what?" Binky looked furious.

"Or Anna Marie will no longer be Cindy's confidant. You know Anna Marie. Self-confidence has never been her strength. I suppose this is just too flattering to turn down."

"I am suddenly so depressed," Binky moaned. She'd forgotten all about her face. "I thought Anna Marie was *our* friend!"

"You can't own people," Lexi pointed out.

"But Cindy is trying to," Angela said.

"She's a controlling personality," Peggy said. "We all see that except for Anna Marie."

Lexi's mind was on the trouble her family had been having with Benjamin and his friend Thomas. There were just some people that bullies liked to pick on, she'd begun to realize. But she'd never known how often it happened until now.

"What can we do about this?" Angela asked. "I *like* Anna Marie. I don't want to lose her as a friend—especially to someone as superficial as Cindy Jarvis."

"First Egg and me, and now Anna Marie," Binky said woefully. "Who's next?"

The fun of the evening had vanished.

Chapter Six

"Jennifer, you have to get those shoes. They are just too great to pass up." Binky talked as she stuffed her mouth with popcorn. Her complexion was still rosy looking but nothing like it had been the first day after her "beauty" mask had been chipped off.

"I don't have the money," Jennifer responded. "How about you, Lexi?"

"No thanks. I have plenty of shoes."

"No one has enough shoes!" Peggy said with a laugh. "Isn't that what Minda says?"

"And if Minda says it, it has to be true," Angela added sarcastically.

The girls had met at the mall for lunch and were now browsing through the stores with no particular purpose in mind.

"I've got to go home soon," Lexi said. "So if anyone of you want *my* opinion on your purchases, you'd better make them soon."

"I'm broke too," Binky said. She crumpled her popcorn bag and threw it into the trash can. "Let's just sit down for a minute. My feet hurt."

They silently watched shoppers walk by, comfortable with one another's company. Occasionally they greeted someone they knew from Cedar River

High. Finally, Lexi stood up. "This is fun, but I've got to go. I—"

"There's Anna Marie!" Peggy hissed. "She's coming our way. Has anyone talked to her since she didn't show up at the slumber party?"

"She's been avoiding me," Jennifer said.

"*All* of us," Angela corrected.

It was Lexi who waved and called out, "Anna Marie, over here! Hi!"

Anna Marie's gaze darted in Lexi's direction. For a moment it appeared that she was going to turn away and pretend she hadn't heard Lexi or seen the other girls. Then, with a resigned sigh the girls could see rather than hear, she walked toward them.

"Shopping?" Lexi asked brightly, pretending she hadn't seen Anna Marie's reluctance.

"A little." The girl seemed nervous. She seemed to want to talk to them and yet seemed to be uncomfortable in their company. "Some shoes."

"We found the coolest pair," Binky began. "Black leather with this great new heel. . . ."

Anna Marie glanced backward over her shoulder.

"Are you listening to me?" Binky noticed Anna Marie's distraction.

"Sure. Black. A new heel." She paused, then started so say something so hurriedly that the words spilled over one another. "Listen, you guys, about the other night. I'm really—"

"There you are!" Cindy's voice floated toward them. She was carrying several packages and looking, as usual, picture perfect. "Anna Marie, I totally need your help carrying all this. I have one more stop before we go to the car. Oh . . . hello."

Cindy glanced at the girls and dismissed them.

"Come on, we have to hurry. We're meeting Roger for dinner at six."

Cindy launched ahead with Anna Marie in tow. Her voice drifted back to the others. "Why were you talking to them? We've discussed this before. You can do better than that, Anna Marie. I've always said . . ."

"Well excuse us for trespassing on your territory," Jennifer muttered.

"Bully," Binky growled.

"Only guys are bullies," Angela said. "Aren't they?"

"She's threatened Anna Marie that to keep *her* friendship, she has to give up *ours*. That's bullying."

"For sure." Binky said this with such wholeheartedness that everyone turned to stare at her.

"I . . . uh . . ."

"What is it, Binky?"

Tears flooded Binky's eyes at Jennifer's question.

"It's just that Egg and I have been so miserable since Roger and Cindy came to school here! You all know how mean Roger is to Egg. He makes fun of him, plays dirty tricks on him, and taunts him all the time. Egg hasn't even said half of what Roger's pulled since he arrived." She paused. "And I haven't said anything about what Cindy's done to me."

"To you? What do you mean?" Angela looked horrified.

Binky snuffled. "She took my homework and hid it one day so that I made a total fool of myself in front of the class. I found it later, stuffed behind some maps. She'd been standing there, laughing at me the whole time."

"That's awful!" Lexi said.

"She does something every day. One day the buckle on my backpack came loose and everything fell on the floor. Egg told me he'd seen Roger and Cindy by my locker the period earlier."

"That's it," Jennifer said. "People should never treat others that way."

"This has got to stop," Peggy agreed.

———

Lexi heard her parents' voices as she came down the stairs for lunch. Her father's tone was agitated, her mother's, soothing.

"Now, Jim, it can't be that bad. I think you are blowing this entire situation out of proportion."

"You didn't know him like I did, Marilyn. People can't change enough to make him likeable. There's no way. Even if he'd had *fifty* years, it couldn't happen."

"You are exaggerating. You know you are. You have to be!" Mrs. Leighton sounded frustrated now.

"Mom? Dad? What's going on?" Lexi entered the room with a worried expression on her face. "Who can't change?"

"Sit down and eat your lunch, Lexi. And don't worry about your father. He's having flashbacks to grade school."

"What your mother means is I'm trying to avoid trouble by not getting involved in a situation that is bound be to a headache."

"Does this have anything to do with your class reunion?" Lexi asked. "You and Mom have been talking about it a lot lately."

Dr. Leighton sighed. "Yes. I got a call this morning from Arlon Henning and Wade Clark. They're going to be in Cedar River today on business, and they want to stop by to discuss our upcoming class reunion. They'd like to start making plans."

"What's wrong with that?" Lexi asked as she pulled a bowl of chicken and rice soup toward her.

"Nothing," Mrs. Leighton said, "except that Arlon Henning is that bully from grade school that your father has talked about."

"And I don't want to see him," Dr. Leighton finished. "But, thanks to your mother, they're coming anyway."

"Jim, I couldn't turn them away when they asked to stop by! That would have been rude."

"Arlon was rude to me plenty of times." Dr. Leighton shook his head. "I know you're right, Marilyn, but I can't help dreading this encounter."

"Maybe he's different now," Lexi said hopefully. She was beginning to grow curious about this man who'd had such an effect on her father.

"I doubt it. Bullies don't grow up. They become locked in childish patterns. Since they lack the proper social skills, they never really learn to have adult relationships."

"Never?"

"Studies have shown that those who were aggressive children commit more crimes, have more driving convictions, and suffer from more alcohol-related problems than the general population."

"Wow!" Lexi's eyes were wide. "I never realized it was so serious. I guess we *should* worry about the boys who are picking on Ben and Thomas!"

"My point exactly," Dr. Leighton said.

"I think we have to hope for the best," Mrs. Leighton offered. "Perhaps you'll wonder why you were once so down on him."

"I hope so," Dr. Leighton said doubtfully. There was a knock on the front door. "Well, here goes!"

Two pleasant-looking men were standing on the other side of the door when Dr. Leighton opened it. Lexi was surprised. She'd expected someone horrible looking after the conversation that had gone on. She couldn't even tell which man might be the one Dad remembered so negatively from his days in school.

"Jim, good to see you," a tall slender man with thinning blond hair and a blue shirt said.

"Wade, nice to see you too."

"Ho, ho, Jim-boy, looks like you made it big after all." The other man had a receding hairline and a slight paunch hanging over his belt. "Never thought you'd do it, but I guess I had to be wrong sometime."

"Hello, Arlon. I see you haven't changed a bit," Dr. Leighton said dryly. "Come in."

He introduced Lexi and her mother and explained that their son Ben was at the neighbor's house and would be home soon. Mrs. Leighton invited them into the living room and asked Lexi to bring coffee and donuts from the kitchen.

Lexi escaped gratefully. She could see what her father had meant. Mr. Clark was a soft-spoken, kind man. But Arlon Henning was another matter entirely. Lexi could hear the men's conversation from the kitchen.

"We've known each other a long time, haven't we, Jim?" Henning's voice boomed. "I remember the first time I saw you. What a little pipsqueak you were! Skinniest little ant on the whole pile. If you had been a fish, I'd have thrown you back." He guffawed loudly.

Lexi gritted her teeth and stacked donuts on a platter. Poor Dad!

"About the reunion," Dr. Leighton began, "tell me your ideas. . . ."

That tactic and the coffee worked for nearly half an hour. With Dr. Leighton and Mr. Clark determined to stay on task, Henning had no real opportunity to continue his insensitive reminiscences.

Mrs. Leighton tiptoed into the kitchen with a rueful expression on her face. "Your father was absolutely right! What a dreadful man. He takes a dig at Jim every time he gets the chance and doesn't even seem to realize he's doing it."

"No wonder Dad didn't want to work with him."

"They seem to be making progress, however. The sooner this is over, the better." Mrs. Leighton turned as the back door opened. "Hi, Ben. Back from Thomas's already?"

"I gotta show Dad what we made," Ben said excitedly. He held a structure in his hand made of Popsicle sticks, glue, and wire. "It's a birdhouse."

Before his mother could stop him, Ben shot into the living room with his arms extended, proudly holding the contraption.

"I made a birdhouse!" he announced. "See?"

Lexi and her mother had followed but paused at the door when the room grew silent. Mr. Clark was looking at Ben's birdhouse with polite interest. Henning, however, was staring at Ben.

Dr. Leighton protectively pulled his son to him. "It's very nice. Where are you and Thomas going to hang it?"

"On the fence. It's for whens."

"I think you mean *wrens*."

"Yeah. Whens."

Dr. Leighton and Mr. Clark both chuckled. Henning kept on staring.

"Gentlemen, this is my son, Benjamin. Ben, Mr. Clark and Mr. Henning are former classmates of mine."

"How do you do?" Ben said politely, more interested in his birdhouse than these dull-looking men.

"Why don't you and Thomas go hang it up?" Dr. Leighton suggested.

Without hesitation, Ben disappeared in the direction of the backyard.

There was a moment of silence before Henning blurted, "What's *wrong* with him?"

"Not a thing," Dr. Leighton said calmly. "He's a perfectly wonderful little boy."

"But he's retarded, isn't he?" Henning made the word sound dirty.

"He has Down's syndrome, if that's what you mean."

"And you kept him? Here at home, I mean? Isn't that hard? If I'd had a kid like that, I would have put him in an institution or something."

Lexi could see her father struggling to hold his temper in check. Henning, completely unaware and uncaring, pressed on. "How do you stand it, Jim? I mean, every day having to look at your own son, knowing he's not right. I suppose I shouldn't admit it, but those kinds of people give me the willies. It's not so bad now, but when he gets older . . ." Henning shuddered. "Bad luck, old man. You must have done something really wrong to deserve this."

Wade Clark stared, horrified, at his companion. His mouth worked but he seemed unable to speak, stunned by the thoughtlessness of the other man.

Dr. Leighton rose to his full six-foot-two-inch height. His fury was barely contained. "My son is plenty 'right,' Arlon. He's a fine boy. Courteous, affectionate, sweet, funny, a loyal friend, and a child I wouldn't exchange for all the 'right' kids in the world. As for Ben being punishment for something I did, that's nonsense. He is a *blessing* to our family."

He crossed the room and firmly took Henning by the arm. "Now I'll have to ask you to leave. I won't be able to work with you on the reunion." He turned to Clark, who was helplessly watching. "Wade, if you'd like some help, I'll offer my office's services to do any mailings you might want to put out. But I'll deal with *you* directly. Arlon and I will not be talking again."

"Always the sensitive one, weren't you, Jim?" Henning sneered. "Haven't grown out of it either."

"No, thankfully I haven't. As you haven't outgrown your *in*sensitivity. I tolerated you as a young person because I had no way to protect myself. But that was then and this is now. Get out of my home, Arlon. I refuse to be bullied anymore."

Lexi watched in amazement as her father gently but firmly kicked his old nemesis out of the house.

Wade Clark trailed behind, but before leaving paused in front of Mrs. Leighton. "Marilyn, I am so sorry. This is the most appalling thing I've ever witnessed. I had no idea. . . ."

"It's not your fault, Wade. Jim knows that. This conflict is old and runs very deep. I'll make sure Jim calls you tomorrow."

"Would you?" Clark looked relieved. "I thought

people grew up by the time they were our age, but I guess not."

"Most do," Mrs. Leighton said gently. "Except the bullies."

Mr. Clark squeezed her hand in mute gratitude and followed the other two men outside.

Lexi peeked out the window. Her father was still talking sternly to Arlon Henning, saying whatever had been building up inside him all these years.

She and her mother were picking up the cups and saucers when he returned to the house.

"Well, that was interesting," Mrs. Leighton commented mildly.

Her husband smiled. "And, despite what Henning said about Ben, cathartic."

"What's that?" Lexi asked.

"Cleansing. Refreshing. Washing away of old pain. I said everything I've needed to say to Henning since we were children."

"Were you mean to him?" Lexi wanted to know. This didn't sound like her dad at all.

"Just honest—and forgiving."

"Forgiving?"

"I've carried a hostility in my heart toward that man for thirty years. Today I was able to see, for the first time, what a weak, confused person he's become. Hardening my heart against him does neither of us any good. I'd never forgiven him for the misery he'd caused me. I'd forgotten all about Matthew 6:14, which says, 'For if you forgive men when they sin against you, your heavenly Father will also forgive you.' I see now that I should have been *praying* for Arlon all along."

"That's pretty hard," Lexi concluded.

"But your dad is right because there's an earlier verse in Matthew that says, 'Love your enemies and pray for those who persecute you, that you may be sons of your Father in heaven. He causes his sun to rise on the evil and the good, and sends rain on the righteous and the unrighteous.' "

"I guess I did have to pray for Minda before we could come to some kind of a truce," Lexi admitted. "And I did feel better."

Dr. Leighton put an arm around his daughter. "Trust me when I say this, Lexi, that if you are in God's will about something, you *always* feel better. It might be hard, but there's a peace that comes with doing what God wishes that can't be duplicated anywhere else. That peace is something hard to explain. It has to be experienced, and once you do, you realize that there's nothing else like it. It's a state you want to be in every moment of every day."

"And you feel that now?"

"About Henning? Yes. We needed to talk. And I needed to forgive. I'm free of him and what he's meant to me. So, in a convoluted kind of way, this was a very *good* morning."

"God works in mysterious ways," Mrs. Leighton quoted. "And now *I'd* better get to work too, or the big mystery around here is going to be what's for dinner tonight!"

Chapter Seven

"There are the guys. Let's walk with them." Binky pointed to Todd and Egg as they walked along the outside wall of the school. "Maybe Todd will have time to give us a ride home today."

"He said he didn't have to work at his brother's garage," Lexi said. "It's about time. He's been filling in for Mike after school so Mike can take a class."

"Yuk. Here comes Roger and his football hangers-on." Binky made a face. "Oh!" Her expression turned from distaste to alarm as Roger met Todd and Egg.

Egg, walking on the outside while Todd remained next to the wall, was talking animatedly using, as he often did, his arms and hands in broad, sweeping motions to illustrate his point. Just as he swung his arms wide apart in some grand gesture, Roger passed him. Egg's arm hit the equipment Roger was carrying, knocking it to the ground.

"Oh, sorry . . ." Egg began, but before he could apologize, Roger took Egg by the front of his shirt and backed him against the wall. His eyes stared down into Egg's wide and startled ones.

"What's the idea, knocking stuff out of my hands?"

"I didn't. I mean, I didn't mean to . . . it was an accident."

"You did it on purpose, McNaughton. You've been out to get me since the day I got here. Let me tell you, you lame little cockroach, it's not going to happen." He ground Egg's back and shoulders into the rough brick. "Don't you ever touch me or any of my stuff again."

"Sorry, Roger. I wasn't looking. . . ."

"I can't help it that you're both blind and dumb." With a jerk, he smacked Egg's head against the wall. Egg cried out involuntarily. "So get over it or plan to pay for it."

"Roger!" Todd's voice was sharp and firm. "He was talking to me. He didn't even see you coming. Lay off."

Roger glared at Todd, but as he did so, took in the body language of Todd's stance—shoulders back, head up, ready, and unafraid. "Don't stick up for him, Winston. He's not worth it."

"I said, *lay off*."

Roger dropped Egg so suddenly that the boy crumpled to the ground in a heap of arms and legs. "You're lucky you've got somebody to protect you, McNaughton. But you can't have your little bodyguard with you all the time. Cross me again and I'll come after you. Wait and see." Roger gave a final kick at the human heap on the ground and turned away, laughing. He swaggered off without looking back.

Binky ran to her brother's side.

His clothing was rumpled and there was a growing knot on the back of his head, but it was Egg's ego that was most badly bruised. He was pale and there were unshed tears in his eyes.

Tiny Binky hauled her brother to his feet and dusted him off. "Don't just lie there, Egg. *Do* something!"

"I can't." The words squeaked through tight lips. Egg hung his head. "He'll pulverize me."

Much as she wanted to protest his statement, Lexi knew it was true. Roger was huge. Strong and mean. Egg wouldn't have a chance if he tried to stand up to the guy.

"What a hothead," Todd muttered. "He's dangerous. He's going to hurt someone if he keeps on reacting like that to things that don't even involve him."

"That's the whole point, isn't it?" Binky murmured angrily. "To hurt someone? Namely Egg?"

"Roger thinks everyone who isn't for him is against him. He intentionally misconstrues innocent gestures. He sees everybody as hostile unless they've pledged some sort of loyalty to him. Plus he enjoys spreading pain and humiliation." Todd stared in the direction Roger had disappeared.

"Maybe now that he's told Egg off, he'll leave him alone," Binky said wishfully.

———

But Binky's hopeful words were just that—words. After the confrontation, the trouble between Egg and Roger grew worse rather than better.

Egg burst into the Hamburger Shack after school the next day looking as though he were going to explode.

"What's wrong?" Angela asked. "You look furious."

"I *am* furious. Roger trashed my bike."

"He did? You saw him?" Lexi gasped.

"Are you kidding? Of course I didn't *see* him. He's too slick for that. But who else would do it? Who else is *strong* enough to do it? It's practically bent in half!" Egg held up a brake wire and some wheel spokes. "And no way is it repairable."

"Why doesn't he leave you alone?" Binky wailed aloud. "You've never done anything to him."

"For some reason Roger thinks it's fun—or funny—to pick on Egg," Todd said. "Although it's beyond me why. Maybe he's got it out of his system now."

"Don't count on it," Egg muttered.

———

"Let's go this way," Egg hissed to Lexi. "Come on."

"Why? It's shorter to our classroom if we go the way we were going. We'll be late if . . ."

"Never mind. Too late," Egg groaned.

Then Lexi saw what he was referring to. Roger and Cindy were walking down the hall in their direction, and there was no way for Egg to escape notice now. Maybe they'd just ignore each other, Lexi thought hopefully.

She was about to sigh with relief as Roger and Cindy passed without even seeming to recognize that she and Egg were in the hallway when suddenly Egg sprawled flat on his face. His nose smacked the tile and his books spun crazily down the hall in three different directions.

"Clumsy," Lexi heard Roger whisper to Cindy. Cindy laughed.

"Egg, are you all right?" Lexi hurried to gather his school books as he shook his head and sat dazedly on the floor. His nose was bleeding and there was a lump the size of an egg swelling over one eye.

"Great. Terrific. Never felt better." Egg's shoulders slumped and he put his head in his hands. "Owwwww!" A finger touched the bruise.

"Here, use these." Lexi pulled a wad of crumpled tissue from the pocket of her jeans. "I'll go get Todd. He can take you to the men's room and help you clean up."

"No, don't." Egg looked furtively around as he scrambled to his feet. "I don't want anyone to know."

"He *tripped* you!"

"Leave it alone, Lexi. He's made me look like a fool enough already. Nobody needs to know about this."

"Are you *protecting* him?" she asked, aghast.

"No. I'm protecting *me*."

―――――

"You know that Old Testament stuff in the Bible?" Binky asked as she swirled her straw in the soda in front of her. She, Lexi, Angela, Jennifer, and Peggy were in the food court at the mall, watching shoppers stroll by.

"Which Old Testament stuff? That's half the Bible." Lexi sounded amused.

"That 'eye for an eye and tooth for a tooth' stuff."

"What about it?"

"I'd like to do that to Roger Mason. He's been so mean to Egg that I'd like to do the same things back to him." Binky thrust the straw so hard into the bottom of the glass that it crumpled.

"Forgiveness is what Jesus preached, Binky, not revenge."

"I know, but revenge against Roger would sure be fun. I'd love to get even with him for some of the things he's done to my brother."

"I know how she feels," Angela said. "Egg has changed since Roger and Cindy came to Cedar River. He's gotten so quiet. It breaks my heart."

"He's scared," Jennifer stated flatly. "And I don't blame him. I've seen Roger in action. Yesterday he knocked the books out of Egg's hands when they were leaving class. One of them hit me in the leg. He's strong and he doesn't care if somebody gets hurt. I said something to Roger and he told me that if I didn't like it, then I'd better quit walking next to Egg because stuff 'just seems to happen' around him."

"I saw it too," Peggy added. "Egg didn't say a word but he looked as though he just shriveled up inside. He's all closed inside himself. I tried to talk to him later, but he wouldn't discuss it. He said that I should forget it because there was nothing that could be done."

"That's the problem," Binky said. "He's given up. He expects Roger to torment him, that it's inevitable and nothing can stop it. I've never seen him like this before."

"A victim," Lexi murmured to herself. "Just like Thomas next door."

"Huh?" Jennifer said. "What are you talking about?"

"Never mind. We've just got to put our heads together and figure out a way to help Egg."

"Hey, Garbage Breath," Roger called from across the chorus room when Egg and Todd entered.

"Can I borrow your math book?"

Egg looked down and kept walking.

"Garbage Breath McNaughton, I'm talking to you." The jeer in Roger's voice was apparent to everyone.

"The name is Egg," Todd responded. "Try using that for a change."

"Okay. If you'd rather be called something that comes out of the backside of a chicken, it's all right with me."

Several of the High Fives burst into laughter. Cindy and—to Lexi's dismay—Anna Marie joined them.

Fortunately, Mrs. Waverly arrived at that moment and Roger grew quiet. Mrs. Waverly had let both him and Cindy know the first day that there would be no nonsense in her presence. Roger was smart enough to know that Mrs. Waverly meant business.

"What was that about?" Todd asked after class when Lexi and Binky had joined them in the hallway. "Since when does Roger want *your* math book?"

"He doesn't. He just wanted to let me know that he knew it was missing—with today's assignment." Egg's voice was flat.

"Where is it?" Binky inquired.

"Gone. Stolen. Probably in Roger's locker, unless he threw it into a garbage can somewhere."

"He *stole* your book and your work?" Lexi gasped. "What are you going to do?"

Egg stared vacantly into space just over her head. "Tell the teacher I didn't get it done, I guess."

"But you *did*! I watched you do it," Binky protested.

"You want me to say a big bully stole it from me?" Egg scoffed. "That would be good. Let everyone know I can't take care of myself."

"But the book . . ."

"I'll have to pay for a new one. I know the ropes. He took one out of my locker last week too."

"And you didn't say anything? Egg, what's wrong with you? You can't let this go on!" Lexi said.

"And I can't stop it. He's like a bulldozer, Lexi. If I fight back he'll just get worse."

"He can't get much worse," Todd pointed out quietly. "I hear what he calls you in the locker room."

Egg hung his head. "Don't tell them." He was referring to the girls.

Todd persisted. "Listen, Egg. It's getting worse, not better. He taunts you every chance he gets. I don't know how you can stand it because *I* can't take hearing him ridicule and insult you anymore."

A look of pain so deep and so all-encompassing that it hurt Lexi to see crossed Egg's features. "Don't get into this, Todd," Egg whispered. *"Just don't."*

"I'm not going to keep my mouth shut any longer. He's ruining the morale of the football team too, with all his behind-the-back comments. No one's said anything because he's supposed to be this great athlete who'll bring us to a conference victory. Well, it's not worth it."

"No!" The single word was so heartfelt and so tragic that it hurt to hear it.

"What's going on, Egg? You've got to tell us." Lexi put a gentle hand on her friend's arm. "We want to help. Let us. Teach us how."

"You can't. You just can't." His expression was forlorn.

"Then tell us why!" Lexi demanded.

"Because when Roger's caught me alone he's threatened stuff a lot worse than he's already done," Egg said flatly. "He means it, and I'm scared."

"Why is Egg being such a wimp about this anyway?" Matt Windsor was saying. "I don't get it. He should just stand up to Roger and tell him to leave him alone."

Todd threw down the wrench he'd been using and leaned against the fender of the car they were working on. Lexi and Jennifer were doing their homework at a nearby table Todd had made out of an old door and some barrels. Doing homework in Mike's garage was something of a tradition with the group by now. Lots of tests had been studied for during an oil change or a tire rotation.

"He's not a wimp—at least not usually." Todd wiped his hands on the cloth hanging out of his back pocket. "Egg's going to have to learn how to handle Roger."

"And how is that?" Jennifer asked. "Because I'd like to learn to handle a bully too. Then maybe I could put Cindy in *her* place."

"Shhh. Here he comes." Lexi pointed to the door.

Egg shuffled in with his hands in his pockets. His shoulders were slumped and he looked defeated.

"How's it going?" Matt asked.

"What do you think? I had to walk six blocks out of my way to get here because Roger and Cindy were at the bus stop on the corner. We cowards don't have an easy life." His words burned with sarcasm and all the pain behind them was glaringly clear.

"Don't let him do this to you," Matt pleaded, "He's messing with your mind. You're a better man than he is."

" 'Man'? Don't you mean 'wimp,' 'geek,' or 'nerd'?" Egg put a finger to his cheek. "What else does he call me? 'Garbage Breath.' That's a good one."

"Quit it!" Matt practically roared.

That got Egg's attention.

"You've got to quit having a pity party for yourself and figure out what to do. So you're scared of him. So what? Everybody is scared sometime. We just need to figure out what to *do* about it."

"Okay, Matt, since you're so smart, you tell me." Egg flopped down on an old chair next to the girls.

"Roger is paranoid, weird, and has a rotten temper," Jennifer said. "And that's not exaggerating."

"My mom's been doing a lot of reading about bullies," Lexi said. "And I've been reading the books too. When you bumped into Roger, he just assumed you did it on purpose. Since he assumes you tried to get him, he wanted to get you back. That's a reason to start a fight for a bully.

"What's more, bullies don't—no, can't—understand how others feel, so they don't even feel guilty about hurting them. And if they don't know how much they hurt someone, they certainly aren't going to feel *guilty* about it. They don't even figure out how much other people despise the way they act!"

"So Roger is insensitive and out of touch with reality. I can agree with that. But that doesn't help me much."

"As long as you are afraid of him, you'll continue to go out of your way to avoid him, miss out on the fun things that happen because you don't want to be near him, and you'll start to think something is wrong with you instead of with him," Lexi said firmly.

"That's what I think already," Egg said glumly. "Besides, it's true. There *must* be something about *me* that's causing this. Roger doesn't pick on everyone. Just me."

"That's not quite true," Jennifer said. "I've seen him start fights with other people. It's just that you get it more often because you don't stand up for yourself."

"What? And get pounded right down to the ground again? Big help that would be."

"No, Egg, I think Jennifer is right. You just don't handle Roger the right way. You don't protect yourself from him, from being exploited." Matt frowned, trying to find a way to express what he wanted to say. "You guys have this bully-victim thing going. Every time Roger picks on you, you act like a whipped puppy because you don't want it to get any worse. That makes Roger think that whatever he's doing is working."

"And you're actually *rewarding* him for what he's doing!" Jennifer added.

"*Rewarding* him? Is *that* what I'm doing?" Egg looked horrified that his friends would even consider saying such a thing. "Then I *am* the problem!"

His jaw squared and a look of determination none of his friends had seen for a long time came into his eyes. "Then I guess, somehow, I'd better find a solution!"

Chapter Eight

"What do you think about Egg and Roger?" Jennifer asked as they walked toward Lexi's house. "I hope we didn't do more harm than good."

"Egg has to understand where Roger is coming from," Lexi said. "Otherwise, he'll never figure out how to handle him."

Jennifer tipped her blond head to the side. "What's that?"

Lexi also stopped walking to listen. "Yelling. Fighting. Sounds like little kids." Then she recognized a familiar note in the cry coming from down the street. "That's *Ben* crying!"

Both girls took off at a run.

When they came to the Leightons' yard, they could see Ben and Thomas huddled against Wiggles' dog house, their arms and hands over their faces. Both were crying. Three stocky older boys were picking rocks out of the flower bed and hurling them and laughing. The pebbles bounced off the roof of the dog house. Ben and Thomas screamed.

It was a horrible sight, Ben and Thomas cowering, terrified, as the other boys found such hilarity in the scene.

"I may not be able to do something about Roger,"

Jennifer muttered, "but I can certainly do something about this." She spurted into action and, surprising the boys, caught two of them by their collars before they had time to escape. The third bolted and disappeared through the next yard and out of sight.

"Let go!" one of the boys demanded.

"No," Jennifer retorted. "Not until you explain just what it is you think you're doing."

"Just having fun, that's all."

She glanced at Ben and Thomas. They were running to Lexi as she held her arms out to them.

"Fun? Do you think they were having fun too?"

"If they weren't such crybabies they would," the taller of the two said. "They're scared of their own shadows."

"Besides," the other boy added, "we weren't going to hurt them. We never even aimed at them. Just the roof of the dog house."

"Do you think they knew that?" Jennifer demanded. "Do you think it felt that way to them?"

"Aw, we were just playing games. Joking around. Teasing, that's all."

"Teasing? I don't find anything funny about it. Saying you were 'just teasing' doesn't make something wrong into something that's okay. It doesn't give you an excuse to be cruel."

"We weren't hurting them," one boy protested. "Anyway, there's nothing you can do about it now."

Jennifer grinned. "That's where you're wrong. I can do plenty."

"You don't even know who we are!" the bigger boy challenged. "So there."

"Wrong again. Don't you remember me? Jennifer Golden? I helped your coach in Little League last summer when his assistant was gone." She grinned unpleasantly. "And even if you've forgotten me, I remember you. Frankie Wertz and Brandon Hammer, right?"

The two boys looked at her in horror. *Caught.*

"If I were you, when I got home, I'd go straight to my room and not make any messes or cause any trouble because you'll want your parents to be very cheerful for the telephone calls they're going to get from these little boys' parents. *They* aren't going to let you get away with this—not anymore."

Frankie and Brandon were finally beginning to realize the enormity of the situation. As Jennifer released them, they scrambled backward pleading, "You don't have to tell our parents. We won't do it again."

"Yeah. We won't even play in this neighborhood."

"Never."

"Honest."

They were still making promises as they hurried away.

Jennifer dusted her hands together with a satisfied smile. "That was fun," she said. "Those were two of the naughtiest boys on the team, and no one ever disciplined them. If someone cared enough about them to make them behave, they'd probably be nice kids."

She grunted as Thomas and Benjamin grabbed her and began to hug her.

"You are awesome!" Thomas finally managed. "You made those mean kids go away!"

"You saved us," Ben said.

Jennifer dropped to the ground and patted the

grass, inviting the pair to join her. "I didn't do anything that you couldn't do."

Thomas shook his head somberly. "Not me. Kids always pick on me."

"They used to pick on me too," Jennifer assured them.

"Not you!"

"Yep. I used to get teased all the time because I wasn't very smart in school."

The boys looked at her in disbelief.

"I couldn't read."

"No way!" Thomas said.

"Have you ever heard of dyslexia?" Jennifer asked. "It's a learning disorder. Letters and numbers get all mixed up on the pages for me. Sometimes I don't know if I'm reading the word 'pot' or 'top.' I'm not dumb, but my learning disorder made it seem like I was. Kids teased me all the time because I couldn't read."

"I can't read 'cause I have Down's syndrome," Ben said. "And I'm not dumb either. I just don't know very much."

Jennifer smiled. "And no one should ever tease you because of it. But kids do tease. You've just got to learn how to handle it. Bullies like kids that they can make cry. They also like it when they can catch you off by yourself where no adults can hear them picking on you. They choose kids who don't have any self-confidence. That means you've got to act like you have it whether you do or not."

"What's shelf confidence?" Ben asked.

"*Self*-confidence is knowing that you are great just the way you are and that no one has a right to make fun of you or hurt you."

"I know why," Ben said, waving his hand in the air. "I'm okay the way I am because God made me and *He doesn't make junk!*"

Jennifer looked at Lexi. "That's the best description I've ever heard of self-confidence."

Lexi laughed and held out her hand. "Come on, guys. We'd better go inside and tell the moms what happened."

Mrs. Watkins and Mrs. Leighton were sitting in the dining room drinking coffee. Mrs. Watkins jumped to her feet when she saw her disheveled young son enter the room.

"Thomas, what happened to you?"

He'd been brave about as long as he could. Tears dripped down Thomas's cheeks.

Ben, seeing his friend cry, promptly began as well.

Lexi and Jennifer quickly sketched out what had occurred.

Mrs. Leighton's frown deepened as the girls talked, but it was Mrs. Watkins' reaction that alarmed them most.

Tears sprung to her eyes and she put a balled fist to her mouth as if to stifle a cry. "Oh, dear. Oh, dear. Oh, dear," she murmured helplessly. "What are we going to do now?"

Lexi, sensing that this was nothing Ben and Thomas should see, suggested the first thing that came to mind. "I'd like a root beer float."

Ben, who was just crying to be social anyway, looked up. "Before supper?"

"Yes. I'd like one *for* supper! Would you and Thomas like to make me one?"

"By ourselves?" Ben gawked at his sister.

"Sure. I'll bet *everyone* would like one. Right, Jennifer?"

"I'll have *two*," she responded, catching on to Lexi's ruse. "Big ones."

"That will be hard. It will take us a long time," Ben said in warning. "And be a little bit messy too."

"Do it anyway. Will you help him, Thomas?"

Thomas glanced at his mother, but the temptation was too much to resist. He nodded and followed Ben into the kitchen. Lexi winced as she heard both refrigerator and freezer doors swing open. She'd probably have to wash the floor tonight in payment for this, but she didn't want to talk to Mrs. Watkins with Thomas in the room—at least not while she was still crying.

"Good idea, Lexi," Mrs. Leighton said, approvingly. "That was quick thinking." Then she turned to Mrs. Watkins. "Please, don't cry. It won't help. We're going to have to discuss this situation and what we can do about it."

"It's just that I can't stand to see Thomas hurt anymore. That poor child has had so many problems. I know he's small for his age and timid, but don't children have the right to be whatever they are without being tormented for it?"

"Of course they do, but sometimes we parents have to give our children some tools to work with too."

"Tools? What do you mean?" Mrs. Watkins quit dabbing at her eyes to look at Mrs. Leighton.

"Social tools. Ways to handle confrontation. Knowing when to walk away. It certainly isn't character or self-esteem building to be picked on. We can teach them that humor can sometimes diffuse an awkward situation. Sometimes assertiveness is necessary.

"We can also provide social opportunities like clubs, classes, or sleepovers that don't lend themselves to bullies. We have to get the message out that keeping kids busy helps. If kids are occupied, they aren't as likely to bully. And," Mrs. Leighton paused for emphasis, "we can have the children stop spending so much time in front of the television set. Many programs are full of bullies. No one needs role models like that!"

Mrs. Watkins looked less teary and more hopeful. Maybe something *could* be done. . . .

Chapter Nine

The note was passed from student to student down one aisle of desks and across another before it reached Lexi. The piece of notebook paper was intricately folded and stained by the touch of many hands. All that could be read on the outside of the note was *PRIVATE: FOR LEXI L.*

Lexi looked up to make sure the teacher had not noticed the note stopping at her desk. She quietly began to work open the elaborate folds of the page. She smoothed it with the palm of her hand but kept her eyes on the blackboard where trigonometry equations were being spun out.

After writing down her assignment for tomorrow and opening her notebook to begin the first problem, Lexi allowed herself a peek at the note. It read:

Lexi,
   Come to my house after school *tonight*. We have to talk! Bring Peggy, Angela, and Jennifer if you want, but *don't* tell Binky or Anna Marie. *They must not know about this.* See you right after school.

Minda

Lexi was so startled, she almost gasped out loud. What could this be about? Minda *never* invited either her or Peggy or Jennifer over after school. Plus, she was usually downright rude to Angela. Immediately, Lexi grew suspicious. What could Minda want with them?

———

"Why us?" Jennifer asked when Lexi gave her the note. "And why not Binky and Anna Marie? I don't get it."

"Who ever gets what's going on in Minda's mind?" Peggy muttered. "I think she's used too much hair dye and it's softened her brain."

"It's scary," Angela added. "Maybe it's a trap and she'll put us in her basement and never let us out."

"Very funny," Lexi said, still puzzled. "I guess the only way we'll know what Minda wants is to go to her house and find out."

———

"Nice place," Angela commented as they pulled into the Hannafords' driveway just off Cedar River's posh Ridge Road. "And a Mercedes Benz in the driveway!"

"It's her dad's," Lexi said. "He lets her drive it because he doesn't get to see her very much since her mom and dad don't live together anymore. I'm sure that's got to be hard on Minda."

"Lexi, you are the most sympathetic person I know. Angela's afraid Minda's going to lock us in the basement and throw away the key while you worry about the poor little girl who had to drive her dad's Mercedes to make herself feel better!" Jennifer kicked at the tire of the car. "Maybe she wants to take us for a drive."

Ignoring her friends' comments, Lexi went to the door and pushed the buzzer. She could hear voices and then footsteps inside the house.

When Minda flung open the door and waved them inside, Jennifer, Peggy, and Angela trailed behind Lexi like curious puppies. They stuck close together and looked with interest around the house.

"We're in the family room," Minda stated. "Grab a soda and follow me."

A fireplace and massive furniture dominated the room. Several of the High Fives were present, including sisters Gina and Tressa Williams and also Rita Leonard, who was wearing, as usual, thick eye makeup and blood red lipstick. Rita, who always looked a little intimidating, seemed even more so today.

"There you are," Rita said by way of a greeting. "You certainly took your time."

"We've only been here a few minutes, Rita," Gina pointed out logically. "They could hardly get here before us!"

"What's the hurry?" Jennifer asked. "And why are we here?"

"Because we need to talk to you. We have to figure out what to do."

"About what?" Jennifer asked, truly puzzled.

"Not 'what.' 'Who.' Cindy Jarvis is driving us nuts, and we have to decide what to do about it." Tressa frowned intently. "I can't believe that girl. She gives females a bad name."

"She's not the only one," Jennifer muttered under her breath. Lexi jabbed her in the rib cage with an elbow.

The High Fives were in a fury about Cindy. Minda kept pacing and chewing on her lower lip as though she were doing some heavy-duty thinking. Finally she spoke. "It's like this. Cindy has been cutting us down, talking about us behind our backs."

"And we won't stand for it anymore!" Gina chimed. "How dare she do that?"

"You do it," Lexi pointed out bravely. Angela and Peggy looked at her in horror.

"That's different," Minda said, not the least bit perturbed by Lexi's honesty. "We've been here forever. Cindy's just moved in and she's already trying to take over."

"Yeah, we were here first." Rita looked even more disgruntled.

"Besides," Minda added reluctantly. "We don't like what she's doing to Binky and Anna Marie."

"But *you* pick on them!" Jennifer blurted.

"I guess so, but this is different." A look of genuine confusion flickered on Minda's face. "We don't like seeing Binky or Anna Marie used like Cindy uses them. She's mean to Binky, and worse yet, she's made Anna Marie her best friend!"

"Now *this* is interesting!" Jennifer muttered under her breath. "The old bullies don't like the new one!"

Minda's petulant face hardened. "It's true, Binky McNaughton is dizzy and drives me nuts sometimes, but I know how *I* felt when Cindy gave me the cold shoulder at camp. I don't want to see her doing that again—even to Binky."

"You mean *you'd* rather be doing it to her instead?" Jennifer asked, her voice honeyed, her meaning clear.

Minda thought about it for a moment, then grinned nastily. "Something like that. I'm used to Binky. I don't want to have to get used to Cindy."

"This is pretty weird," Lexi pointed out. "You certainly aren't planning to help Binky for the right reasons."

"But, at this point, I think we should take all the help we can get," Peggy pointed out logically. "Cindy is tormenting Binky. Roger is coming down hard on Egg. They're both miserable. If we don't try to put a stop to their thoughtless behavior, even more kids are going to suffer. They aren't going to change once Binky and Egg's lives have been ruined, are they?"

"When you put it that way . . ." Lexi was reluctant.

"Look at it this way," Gina said. Until she spoke, the other High Fives had been letting Minda do most of the talking. "Both Binky and Anna Marie are pretty torn up. We can all see it. Anna Marie is your friend. She doesn't like ignoring you like Cindy asks. And Binky's too soft to stop Cindy from hurting her. Once Cindy 'conquers' them, who will she be on to next? Me? Tressa? Minda? We've got to nip this problem in the bud."

"This is crazy!" Lexi blurted. "The High Fives *are* usually our problem!"

Minda gave her a disgusted look. "And we probably will be again, but for now, we want to help. Are you with us or not?"

Lexi realized that somewhere in the self-centered hearts of the High Fives there was a soft spot for their friends that was worth nurturing. "You aren't planning anything mean, are you? You can't sink to Cindy's level."

"Have you talked to Anna Marie lately?" Minda asked slyly. "I mean, really talked?"

"Not exactly," Lexi admitted.

"No one has," Peggy added. "No one can get close to her because Cindy's always right beside her chasing us away."

"Even Cindy can't be with Anna Marie every hour of the day!" Lexi protested.

"Can't she?" Jennifer asked. "I've called her twice. We've talked for a few seconds and then call waiting beeps in. It's always Cindy, and Anna Marie says she has to hang up. The way it sounded to me was that Anna Marie didn't even want Cindy to know she was talking to someone else on the phone."

"I'd love to fix that Cindy Jarvis," Rita muttered.

"Fix? What's that supposed to mean?" The conversation made Lexi uneasy.

"You worry too much, Lexi," Minda said. "Besides, if we don't stop what's happening, that means we're condoning it."

"You have to promise me something," Lexi said urgently. "Please?"

"What's that?"

"You can't do anything hurtful. I know bullies should be stopped. I just don't want *you* to stop Cindy by being a bigger bully than she is. There's a verse in Proverbs that says—"

"I knew she'd get the Bible in here somewhere," Tressa groaned.

Lexi continued, undaunted, "Proverbs 16:7 says, 'When a man's ways are pleasing to the Lord, he makes even his enemies live at peace with him.' "

"Even Cindy?"

"Yes, even Cindy."

"You know, Lexi, if that's true and what you say actually works, then I'm going to have to take another look at your religion stuff," Minda said.

As she thought about the conversation later, Lexi wondered how God would work this one out. She knew He could take lives and turn them around in a heartbeat. It was a pretty creative God she worshiped, Lexi thought, glad to turn this whole problem over to Him.

———

"What do you think of that?" Jennifer asked after they'd left Minda's house. "It blows me away to think that Minda the Bully is bugged by Cindy the Bully!"

"I was talking to Todd and Egg about girls who were bullies and at first they made fun of me, saying that guys were the worst bullies because they could hurt you physically," commented Lexi.

"Ha!" Jennifer scoffed. "That shows how much they know. Girls can be just as mean as guys in their own way. Bullies want to hurt people, and there are lots of ways to do that."

"Like spreading awful rumors about someone so that others will reject them," Peggy suggested. "Or giving someone the 'silent treatment' to get even with them."

"I always hated it in grade school when someone would say, 'You can't come to my party unless you do this or that,' " Lexi admitted.

"Or how about that line, 'If you're going to be her friend, you can't be mine'?" Peggy said. "Cindy's using that old grade-school line on Anna Marie right now!"

"Why do we let it get to us?" Jennifer puzzled. "We should just ignore bullies!"

"It works because we *want* friends. They are important to us. If friends didn't matter, then the bullies would find some other way to manipulate us."

"Cindy picked Anna Marie as her friend because she could control her," Jennifer concluded. "Anna Marie is totally nonaggressive. She's easy to push around."

Peggy frowned. "She's had enough problems already. She doesn't need this."

"Our conversation with the High Fives didn't make me feel very good about myself," Lexi admitted thoughtfully. "It took Minda, Gina, and Tressa to make me realize that bullying *isn't* something that happens between just two people. Having a crowd around when bullying happens insures that everyone else will know who's boss. We've almost stopped talking to Anna Marie because that's what Cindy wants. Pretty soon, Anna Marie *won't* have any friends but Cindy—and that's not the worst of it!"

"Then what is?" Jennifer asked. "That sounds pretty bad to me!"

"Even if Anna Marie does decide to get away

from Cindy, it might be too late." Lexi formed her words carefully. "It's like Ben's friend Thomas. He's always been picked on by bigger, meaner boys. His parents have even come to *expect* that it will happen. Even if Thomas did change, everyone around him would still assume that he's a weak, frightened little kid. People would see him the same way as they had before he changed. We assume that once someone is a victim, he'll always be one."

"All I can say is that this is both complicated and weird," Jennifer stated. "Not only are we trying to figure out what to do about bullies, but we're actually agreeing with Minda—our *own* personal neighborhood bully!"

"Weird," Peggy agreed. "Very, very weird."

Chapter Ten

"Where's Jennifer tonight?" Binky asked. She, Lexi, and Angela were studying at Peggy's house. "I thought she said she was coming over."

"She was." Peggy stretched as she answered. "But then she called later to say that she had a baby-sitting job and wouldn't be here."

Binky's eyes narrowed suspiciously. "It's not . . ."

"It is," Peggy said glumly.

"What are you talking about?" Angela demanded.

"Jennifer's baby-sitting for *Ryan* again." Peggy said the name as though it were an infectious disease instead of a child.

"I thought she'd never go back." Binky looked shocked. "He was horrible."

"What made her change her mind?" Angela asked.

"She's been talking to my mom, for one thing," Lexi said. "Mom's been doing so much reading on the subject that she's practically an expert."

"It would take an expert to handle that child," Peggy agreed. She glanced at the clock. "I wonder how Jennifer is doing?"

"Let's go see," Binky suggested. "I need a break anyway. This is too boring for words and she's not very far away."

"I don't know." Angela was reluctant. "I hate to see anyone suffer—especially Jennifer."

"That's when she needs us most!" Binky closed her book decisively. "Let's go."

The house was quiet as they approached—no screaming banshee swinging from the trees and no Jennifer, red-eyed and pulling at her hair in frustration. Lexi tapped gently on the door and the girls could hear footsteps approaching.

"Hi!" Jennifer's face was wreathed in smiles. "Look, Ryan, we've got company!"

The little boy appeared behind Jennifer, freshly scrubbed and wearing action-hero pajamas. His hair was still damp from his bath and he carried a tattered stuffed dog.

"What do we say to our company, Ryan?" Jennifer prodded.

He put his thumb in his mouth and stared at her blankly.

"I guess that was too much to hope for," Jennifer said softly. "Come on in."

Binky entered looking dazedly to her right and to her left as if she'd just landed in a different dimension. "I don't get it. What happened here? It's so quiet. *He's* so . . ."

"Great, isn't it?" Jennifer ruffled Ryan's hair. "We've come to a little agreement, Ryan and I."

"How?" Angela, too, was amazed.

"Lexi's mom gave me some tips." She turned to the little boy. "You were very good for your bath.

That means it's snack time. Do you want to put chips in a bowl for us?"

"And dip?" Ryan asked suspiciously.

"Sure. We'll have sodas too. No caffeine for you, though."

He slid off the couch and headed for the kitchen. He looked back twice as if to indicate he didn't quite know what to do with all this trust Jennifer was showing in him. With a resigned sigh, he disappeared into the next room.

"Tell us what happened! He's a changed kid!" Peggy said.

"Not totally. We've just come to a truce. Mrs. Leighton told me that kids who aren't corrected and made to behave when they're young might never stop their bullying behavior. She says, 'Bullies are made, not born.' When I thought about it for a while, I decided that it would be a shame to let Ryan grow up the way he was going, so she gave me a few hints to try."

"And he's acting like this?" Binky was amazed.

"It's new to him yet, but I think he's getting the idea that he can't bully me anymore. He's also realizing that I'm much more *fun* when he behaves."

"What do you do?"

"I won't tolerate any sort of bullying or bad behavior. I don't get mad or threaten him and I don't do anything to him physically other than take away privileges or make him have a 'time out' in a chair till he calms down. *Every time* he breaks one of the rules, this happens. Mrs. Leighton said I had to be consistent so that Ryan knows that I won't tolerate any bullying behavior—ever."

"That sounds like a lot of work for you," Binky commented.

"It is, but believe me, it's easier than chasing him around trying to make him settle down once he's all stirred up. Besides, if he's good, we have fun. We paint or make clay sculptures or draw pictures. Ryan's a good little artist and likes it when we paint together. I think he's learning that it can be even more fun than being a bully."

"I wish Roger and Cindy had learned that," Binky said. Her voice was forlorn and everyone knew she was thinking about Egg and Anna Marie.

"I guess they got stuck in a nasty stage," Angela concluded. "I wonder if there's any way to 'unstick' them now."

"Can you tell me more about this handling a bully stuff?" Binky asked thoughtfully. "I think this is what Egg needs to hear."

———

"Let's watch the guys practice football tonight," Peggy suggested. "We haven't done that for a while."

"Todd said it would be a short practice," Lexi added. "I'll ask him if he can give us a ride home afterward. We can catch up with him after he leaves the locker room to go to the field."

That was how Lexi, Peggy, Binky, and Jennifer came to be standing just outside the players' door when Roger and Egg's disagreement began.

Egg came through the door first, hauling a batch of water bottles and sporting a bunch of towels on one shoulder. He was red-faced and sweating and looked miserable. Two or three players passed him, each tossing another towel onto his shoulder. It wasn't until Roger came out, however, that the trouble began.

If Lexi had not been watching so closely, she never would have seen the movement that caused the explosion.

As he came around Egg, Roger, too, tossed a towel on Egg's shoulder. At the same moment, Roger's knee, in heaving padding, bent in behind Egg's. Surprised and unprepared for the blow, Egg's knees buckled and he dropped to the ground, water bottles and towels slipping in every direction.

"Watch it, clumsy!" Roger yelped. He acted as though he'd had nothing to do with the fall.

"I didn't . . ." It took Egg a moment to gather his wits about him.

"I don't want to drink out of a water bottle that's been rolling around on the ground. I know you're too lame to play football, but you're the first person I've ever seen too dumb to be a water boy!" Roger laughed heartily at his own humorless joke.

Egg sputtered a protest as he scrambled to his feet. "You did it, Mason, and you know it."

Roger's mood turned lightning quick from mocking to furious. He grabbed Egg by the shirt collar and slammed him against the school's brick wall. "Are you accusing me of tripping you? *You?* Clumsy, flat-footed, brain-dead Egg McNaughton? Why, you little creep. . . ."

It was Todd at Roger's elbow who stopped the exchange.

"Cool it, Roger. Let Egg go." Todd's voice was low and firm.

Roger turned to him with angry eyes, but when

he saw Todd, large and impressive in his own football gear, he dropped his hand. "Are you defending this mouse, Winston? Haven't you got any other charity work to do? Why don't you save somebody *worth* saving?"

Todd smiled coolly. "Egg is a friend of mine and I'd like him to stay in one piece."

"There's no accounting for taste," Roger grumbled, but he allowed Todd to lead him away.

It wasn't until the boys were almost to the football field that the girls realized that Egg had slipped away.

"I can't find him," Matt told Binky. "He's not in the locker room. I looked everywhere." He flushed. "Even the closets."

"Where could he have gone?" Binky wailed. "He's *never* run away before! Coach Drummond is looking for him."

"He just needed some time to pull himself together," Matt said. "It's not easy getting humiliated in front of an entire football team—and his girlfriend."

Angela flushed angrily. She looked as miserable as Binky. They all did. Roger had gone too far this time, but no one knew quite what to do about it.

Just then Todd emerged from the locker room, his hair damp and his jacket draped casually over one shoulder. "Where's Egg?"

"We can't find him," Lexi said softly. "Matt has been helping us search. He's vanished. I'm worried about him, Todd."

"So am I." A frown marred his forehead. "But I think I might know where he's hiding."

Todd led them through the school to the *Cedar*

River Review room, where the school paper was put together. The hallway was dark and the door to the *Review* was locked. Todd knocked anyway.

He put his ear to the door and listened intently, then he knocked again. "Come on, Egg. We know you're in there. You can't stay there forever."

As the others watched in amazement, the door glided open. Egg was framed in the doorway, anguish glistening on his features. "How'd you know I was here?"

"I know you have a key," Todd said softly as he guided Egg back into the room. "And I know that Roger Mason wouldn't darken the doorstep of a place that might involve extra work. It just made sense."

"Egg?" It was Tim Anders, poking his head around the doorjamb. "Are you okay? I heard. . . ."

"Come on in," Todd invited. "We need your help."

Egg glared at Todd suspiciously. "With what? Picking up the pieces of my shattered ego? Sorry. Too late. They are scattered so far that no one will ever be able to put it back together again." Egg was fighting back tears. "I just don't get it. I stay out of his way. I don't look him in the eye. I don't talk to his girlfriend or touch his stuff. Why can't he just leave me alone?"

"Maybe *because* of those things," Matt said bluntly.

"Huh?" Egg looked startled.

"In Roger's eyes, you are a real wimp," Matt continued. "Weak. Scared. Just the kind of guy Roger likes to pick on because he knows he can always win."

"Well, he can. There's no way I could fight Roger. He'd pound me."

"I don't mean physical fighting," Matt said. His air of authority told everyone that he was speaking from personal experience. "You've got to deal with Roger on a psychological level."

"I can't out-think him either," Egg said morosely. "My brain goes blank when I see him coming."

"Victim mentality," Lexi said.

"That's me." Egg stirred a little in his seat. "Maybe I should change schools."

"And be like Thomas?" Lexi blurted.

"Who's that?"

"Our little neighbor boy. His parents moved to get away from some bullies, but new ones have already found him."

"That would be just my luck," Egg groaned.

"Don't give up now," Todd advised. "You just don't know how to handle Roger, that's all."

"And how am I supposed to learn? After all, I've known him since first grade. If I haven't figured it out by now, I doubt that I will."

"We'll help you." Matt's words were firm. Todd and Tim nodded.

"First thing you have to do is quit hiding," Tim advised. "I'm not very big, but Roger leaves me alone."

"Good for you," Egg said bitterly.

"Really. I see you scooting off down the hall every time Roger's anywhere in the vicinity. You look like a scared rabbit."

"I *am* a scared rabbit."

"So pretend you're not. He can't give you trouble

every time he sees you. Put your chin up and walk past him. You'll be okay as long as there are teachers around—or us." Tim indicated Matt and Todd. "Practice not being scared. Roger loves to pick on you because you *are* afraid."

"Tim's right," Matt added. "You can decide when it's a good idea not to be near Roger. Then leave. But don't run at first sight of him."

"I just don't understand why we can't get along. . . ." Egg's voice trailed away miserably.

"Why should you?" Jennifer asked.

Egg looked up, puzzled.

"It's not realistic to expect that *everyone* will like you. None of us are liked by every single person in school. Take Lexi, for example."

Lexi looked up as Jennifer continued. "Lots of people like her, but some think she's a 'goody-two-shoes.' If she tried to please those people, others wouldn't like the change. Who's she going to please? Certainly not everyone."

Egg took that bit of information thoughtfully.

"What I'm trying to say is that you shouldn't *care* if Roger likes you or not. You try your best to be a good person. You have friends who love and appreciate you. Isn't that enough?"

"He wouldn't have to like me if he'd just leave me alone," Egg conceded.

"That's fair," Todd said. "Lots of kids feel that way about Roger."

"They do?"

"Sure. You've been so involved with your own feelings and problems that you haven't even noticed what he does to others. Every guy in the sophomore class feels just like you do. Roger doesn't pick on upper classmen because they might stand up for themselves, but the under classmen are fair game to him."

"I didn't realize . . ." Egg considered what the boys were telling him. "So what should I do?"

"First, start looking confident even when you aren't. Roger can practically *smell* it when you're afraid." Todd smiled a little. "Then, count on us."

"What do you mean?" Egg was confused.

"I think it's time that Roger realized you have friends who don't approve of the way he's treating you."

"Sorry. I didn't see you." Cindy smirked as she ran full force into Binky carrying her lunch tray. She'd had to go out of her way to do so. "You really made a mess."

Chocolate pudding and taco fixings had spilled to the floor. Lunchroom policy was that if a student made a mess, she cleaned it up. There was a dust pan, mop, and paper towels available for just such occurrences.

"I think *you* should clean it up."

Cindy looked up sharply at the sound of Minda's voice as she, Rita, Gina, and Tressa flanked Binky.

"We noticed that *you* hit Binky, not the other way around," Rita said sweetly. "So we're sure you'll want to clean it up."

Cindy gave a sound of disgust but didn't argue. The High Fives had a reputation for being influential around the school and also for being troublesome if crossed.

Cindy turned to Anna Marie who stood behind

her and said, "Anna Marie, clean it up for me, will you?"

"Wait a minute!" Gina piped in with true irritation in her voice. "She doesn't have anything to do with this!"

"And neither do you," Cindy snapped. "Anna Marie, do it."

Anna Marie made a move to put her tray down on a nearby table.

"Stop that!" Minda said sharply. "You aren't her slave. She made the mess, she can clean it up."

"What does it matter who does it?" Cindy snapped. "She doesn't mind."

"But *we* do. We don't like the way you treat her," Tressa said.

"Why? I doubt you're all that crazy about her," Cindy rejoined. Anna Marie looked miserable.

"At least we don't treat her like she's our slave. And from now on, we won't let *you* either." Minda turned to Anna Marie. "Why don't you sit with Lexi and Binky? We'll make sure Cindy gets this mess cleared up."

Anna Marie, not knowing what to do and anxious to be out of the middle of the confrontation, took the place Lexi had been holding for her.

Cindy turned to Minda with a snarl.

At that moment, Mrs. Waverly, whose turn it was to oversee the lunchroom, walked up to the group. It was apparent that she'd seen and heard the entire exchange.

"Problems?" she asked. Then, before anyone could answer, she turned to Cindy. "Where were you planning to sit? I'll take your tray so you are free to mop up the mess."

Cindy's mouth worked, but no sound came out.

Gently, Mrs. Waverly took the tray. She set it down on a table away from Binky and the others.

When Cindy stomped off to get the mop, Mrs. Waverly turned to Minda and her friends. "Thank you, girls, for helping Binky. Bullying behavior is unacceptable at any time. I'm glad you realize that." She gave them a knowing and perceptive look. "And I'm sure you'll remember that for yourselves in the future as well."

She patted Minda's arm. "Go and eat. I'll help Cindy."

"Wow!" Binky breathed. "Points for Mrs. Waverly! She managed to put *both* Cindy and the High Fives in their place. Awesome."

"Do you think Cindy will get the message?" Anna Marie's voice was timid, close to tears.

Lexi put her hand on Anna Marie's arm. "I think she's got it already."

Anna Marie looked as though she were going to cry. "I don't want to be in the middle of this. I miss you guys so much, but Cindy said that if I were your friend . . ."

"That you couldn't be *hers*?"

Anna Marie nodded miserably. "She can be nice. She really can. It's just that she can't understand that I can be a friend to more than one person."

"I don't see why you are willing to accept that," Binky said bluntly. "Why can't you tell her it's too much to ask? You've been our friend much longer!"

Lexi glanced at Anna Marie's guilty face and understood. "Because it's very flattering to be picked out as a 'best friend' to someone who's as new and interesting as Cindy. Her boyfriend is a big jock who's going to save the football team from itself. She's pretty and rich and wears all the right clothes—"

Anna Marie interrupted before Lexi could finish. "And no one has ever picked *me* out like that before."

Binky reached out and touched Anna Marie's hand. "I'm sorry."

"Sorry? Why? You didn't do anything to me." Anna Marie's expression was puzzled.

"I didn't do anything to make you feel special, either. I took you for granted. We all did. We didn't tell you that you matter to us, that your friendship is important. That we'd miss it if you weren't there. That was a mistake." Binky looked around at the group. "I learned something from this. I'm going to *tell* my friends how much they mean to me instead of just assuming they can read my mind. You can be Cindy's friend if you want to, but I want you to be my friend too."

A glow radiated from Anna Marie's smiling face. "Thank you, Binky. If I'd heard that before, maybe I'd have been brave enough to tell Cindy that myself. Now I guess Cindy's going to have to choose— let me be with my friends or leave me alone entirely."

"Go, girl!" Jennifer piped. "You tell her!"

Lexi leaned to hug Anna Marie. "Welcome back."

None of them paid any attention to Cindy, who glowered as she wiped chocolate pudding off the cafeteria tile.

Chapter Eleven

Cindy Jarvis was lying low. The confrontation with the High Fives and Mrs. Waverly had apparently caused her to decide that Anna Marie wasn't worth her efforts any longer. She needed someone more passive to control—and someone with fewer friends to stand up for her.

Anna Marie was primarily relieved, but it was bittersweet.

"I *did* like Cindy some of the time," she told Lexi as they made their way down the hall. "When we were alone and she knew she had my complete attention, she could be both fun and funny. She's very smart, you know. Except where relationships are concerned."

"Bullies just don't get it," Lexi commented. "And as long as we allow ourselves to be bullied, there won't be an end to the problem. We can hope Cindy will realize that trying to control others just won't work here anymore. It's not all bad news, though. In fact, I think we had some pretty *good* news from Thomas's mom yesterday."

"Ben's friend?"

"Yes. She's been hanging out with my mother a lot lately, and you know how my mom is. Once she gets an idea about how to solve a problem, she doesn't give up until she finds a way. She's been taking Mrs. Watkins with her to school board and teachers' meetings to talk about the importance of preparing children for life.

"She's finally beginning to understand why Thomas has such trouble. Bullies always pick on kids younger and weaker—kids who can't fight back. Usually those kids are more cautious, quiet, and nonaggressive than others. They practically radiate fear and anxiety in uncomfortable situations. Unfortunately, bullies seem to have an innate sense of weakness when looking for victims."

"The kid sounds like a wimp," Anna Marie said bluntly. "Like me. And if I learned only one thing from this business with Cindy, I learned that victims are as unpopular as bullies are. I just *knew* that everyone noticed I wasn't sticking up for myself and respected me less because of it. I *wanted* things to be different, but I didn't know what to do. I felt so isolated from everyone, so rejected. . . ."

Tears sprang to Anna Marie's eyes. "I never want to go through anything like that again."

"And now, knowing what you know, you won't have to," Lexi said. "That's the good news for Thomas, too. His mom has realized that in order to help Thomas she had to quit protecting him. Instead of making sure he never sees conflict, she's trying to teach him ways to handle it and to give him confidence so he can manage without her around."

"Weird, isn't it?" Anna Marie observed. "Overprotecting a child hurts him by not giving him the opportunity to learn how to avoid being exploited by other kids. It must be hard to be a parent."

"Almost as hard as it is to be a kid," Lexi said with a smile.

They walked toward the front door of the school in silence.

The *Cedar River Review* staff was holding a fund-raiser to earn money to send several of the staff to a high school writing conference. Businesses had donated gifts ranging from movie tickets with free soda and popcorn to name-brand sweat shirts, certificates for restaurants, and best of all, from Mike Winston's garage, a car!

Granted, it was a used—very used—vehicle, but Mike had overhauled it, taken the dings and dents out of the finish, and polished it to a high sheen. Ticket sales were booming. "I figure, even if I won it," Minda was saying to Matt and Tim as she purchased a book of tickets, "I could sell it and get spending money for the conference. It's a win/win deal for me. I get the trip for sure because we're earning so much money on the ticket sales."

Roger Mason was standing near the table eyeing the potential prizes and the tickets Egg was holding. "So how do they figure out who gets the sweat shirt and who gets the car?"

"Here's a list of the order the winning tickets will be drawn." Egg pushed a sheet of paper toward Roger but didn't meet his gaze. "The last ticket drawn will be for the car. You have to be here to win."

Roger glanced at the sheet and his face darkened. "That's the date I'm being interviewed for a football scholarship at the state university. There's no way I'll be back for the drawing!"

"Sorry. Do you want to buy some tickets anyway, just to support the *Review*?" Egg's sentence ended with a strangled sound as Roger plucked him out of his chair and dragged him across the table.

"Change the date," Roger ordered. "You're in charge of this thing. Fix it."

Egg had both hands on Roger's wrists, trying to get himself out of the stranglehold. When Roger let go, Egg dropped to the tabletop in a tangle of arms, legs, and papers.

With as much dignity as he could muster, Egg straightened his shirt and squared his shoulders. "I can't do that. The date is set."

"It's not fair."

"Somebody is bound to miss this, no matter what night we choose. Guess that night it will be you."

"Why, you little—"

"Chill out, Roger, you wouldn't want that car anyway. There's no guarantee it will even start." Egg's unexpected attempt at diffusing the situation with humor caused Roger to give a look of astonishment.

He stared at Egg curiously but would not be deterred. "You just don't want me to have a chance at that car. I'll bet you fixed that date. You knew I had interviews."

"Get a life, Roger." Egg was uncharacteristically assertive. "There are lots more important things to think about than winning a four-hundred-dollar car."

"I don't have to take this . . ." Roger began.

"No, *I* don't have to take it. Not anymore. I'm tired of being pushed around by you, so I quit." Egg handed Tim the tickets. "Here, you sell them for a while. I've got things to do." With that, Egg strode down the hallway.

Roger started after him but came up short when Matt and Todd, who'd observed the altercation, stepped in front of him.

"Let him go," Matt said softly.

"I will not!" Roger's face grew red.

"I think you will. Egg's right. He doesn't have to be pushed around by you. No one does."

"So he needs bodyguards to protect him?" Roger sneered.

"No, but he has *friends*." Matt and Todd were like an implacable wall with their arms crossed, their expressions serious. Even Roger, large as he was, knew better than to argue.

"You just wait. You can't protect your scrawny little friend all the time. I'll get him. You'll see."

"Don't count on it."

The guys spun around to see Mrs. Waverly, hands on her hips, tapping the floor with the toe of one shoe.

"Mrs. Waverly! I . . . uh . . ."

"I heard your threat, Roger. There's no use trying to take it back now."

"I was just kidding around, Mrs. Waverly. No big deal."

"Todd, Matt, did Roger's words seem like kidding around to you?"

"No, ma'am. Not to Egg either," Matt muttered.

"You can't wash away the cruelty in your words by insisting you were kidding," Mrs. Waverly told Roger.

Roger's full face convulsed with anger. "What's

the deal, anyway? How come everybody's sticking up for McNaughton all of a sudden? Who died and made him important?"

Mrs. Waverly's expression tightened. "Egg's always been important here, just as every student is. Actually, Egg is not the issue. We've had several calls from parents and comments by students that *you* have been causing trouble, Roger."

"Me? Who's been talking about me?" Roger looked both amazed and furious.

Mrs. Waverly ignored the question. "At the school board meeting this week, a new committee was appointed to deal with certain negative behaviors throughout the school system. Bullying is one of them."

Roger's expression relaxed and he burst out laughing. "Bullying? You're kidding, right?"

"Not at all. The new citizenship committee feels that behavior is the cause of a good share of the problems in this or any school." She glanced at her watch. "I think we can still catch Egg so you can apologize to him before—"

"Apologize? To Garbage Breath? No way." Roger started to walk away.

"Mr. Mason." Mrs. Waverly's normally soft voice was sharp, compelling Roger to turn around. "You will come with me, please."

Roger stared at her in disbelief.

"Now. If I can't convince you to offer an apology, then perhaps someone in the administration can."

Roger was sputtering, his cheeks burning. "I'm not . . . I won't!"

"You *will*. If not, the issue becomes whether or not you will be able to play football for this school.

Unbecoming conduct, disobeying teachers . . ." Mrs. Waverly walked away then, confident Roger would follow.

And follow he did, his demeanor changed. "You wouldn't let them kick me off the team just because McNaughton is a wimp, would you? I can leave him alone. He's nothing to me anyway."

Several of the students who'd been present for Roger's humiliation began to cheer and clap.

Todd whistled under his breath after they'd disappeared. "She's *tough*."

"Awesome," Lexi agreed. "I'll bet nobody's ever bullied *her*."

"It's weird," Tim murmured, "but suddenly I feel . . . free."

"He might be great for the football team, but he's no hero otherwise," Angela said. Several students nodded in agreement.

A small sound caught Lexi's attention then and she turned toward it. Cindy Jarvis was standing in the corner, listening and watching. How much had she heard and seen?

Plenty, Lexi guessed, by the look on her face. Cindy held her knuckles to her lips as if to press back tears. A wave of pity flooded through Lexi as it occurred to her that neither Cindy nor Roger had had any idea how little the kids at Cedar River had liked them or their insensitivity to others. They were both clueless as to how to deal with people properly. Cindy might be beautiful and rich. Roger might be a great athlete. But so far they'd proven themselves to be pretty lousy friends.

Lexi watched Cindy slink off and decided that the verse in the Bible that asked her to pray for her enemies would probably apply in a case like this.

Peggy, Lexi, Binky, Angela, Anna Marie, and Jennifer found the guys in the parking lot looking under the hood of Todd's old car. The guys were discussing what had happened inside with Roger and Mrs. Waverly and giving Egg all the gory details he'd missed by walking away from Roger.

"You were doing really well, Egg," Todd was saying. "You handled him the way bullies should be handled—with humor, with self-confidence, and finally by refusing to take what he was trying to dish out."

"But by walking away I missed all the fireworks," Egg pointed out. "I wish I could have seen Mrs. Waverly in action."

"She's pretty cool," Matt admitted.

"What are you going to do when Roger apologizes to you?" Tim asked.

"I'm not holding my breath," Egg said. "But if he does, I guess I'll just accept his apology."

"And not rub his face in it?" Tim sounded horrified. "I'd want to get even, if I were you!"

"Nah. I know how that feels. It might be fun for a minute, but I wouldn't feel good later. Roger can be as rotten as he wants, but I don't want to sink to that. After all, I have to live with myself."

Impulsively, Lexi gave Egg a squeeze. "You are so cool, Eggo."

Egg blushed. "Really? Nobody's *ever* said that about me before!"

Anna Marie gave a breathy sigh. "That tells me what *I* have to do."

The kids turned to look at her curiously. "What's that?"

"Forgive Cindy, too. She really isn't all bad. I did feel manipulated by her and even a little afraid of what she might do or say if I *didn't* listen to her, but it was kind of flattering that she picked *me* as her friend." A sadness flickered on her face. "She's dropped me like a hot potato now. I don't even exist to her anymore. I guess that tells me how good a friend I really was to her."

They gathered at the Hamburger Shack after school for sodas to celebrate another winning football game. Todd came late, his hair still wet from the shower.

"Congratulations!" Jennifer yelled.

Todd waved the compliment away. "Roger was the amazing one. He's a real athlete." He sank down on the booth next to Lexi. "Too bad he's making noises about transferring."

"Again?" Binky sounded surprised. "Now that he's been acting almost human for a change?"

"He and Cindy have been keeping a pretty low profile since that confrontation with Mrs. Waverly. News of that got all over school, and it seemed to empower everyone not to take his bullying anymore. I don't think he likes not being center stage or not being able to intimidate or manipulate people any longer."

"I suppose if Roger goes, Cindy will, too," Anna Marie said softly.

"They are made for each other," Jennifer said bluntly. "Two of a kind."

"You aren't still feeling bad about her, are you, Anna Marie?" Binky asked.

"Sort of. For a while she really made me feel important. I know it's dumb, but that part of our friendship felt good. It sounds silly, but it's not easy to see her with her new best friend." Cindy had chosen a sophomore girl this time. They were together constantly.

"The new girl is even quieter than me," Anna Marie continued. "Oh, well, better her than me. I'm glad it's over."

"Bullying doesn't work so well in our school these days," Peggy said. "Not since the new school policies and the education program they've put in place. The faculty is pretty enthusiastic about not allowing that kind of garbage to happen anymore."

"And Lexi's mom is partly to thank for that," Jennifer said. "I heard about all those meetings she attended. Awesome."

Egg, who'd been very quiet, cleared his throat. "I'd like to say something."

All heads turned his way.

"I just want to say thank-you," he stammered. "I couldn't have ever stood up to Roger without your help. You guys supported me. You let Roger know that if he picked on me he'd have to answer to you. Knowing you all cared about me made me stronger. Thanks."

Egg's cheeks burned with embarrassment and the speech made him choke with emotion. "Now can we forget this whole thing?"

"Forget what?" Todd said cheerfully. "I can't even remember what we were talking about."

"Me either," Matt added.

Everyone else nodded.

Relief showed on Egg's face.

It was over. No matter what Roger and Cindy did now, they couldn't hurt any of them anymore. They would defend one another. They were friends. Finally, things could go back to normal. And normal was the best way for things to be.

Could things ever get so bad at home that Lexi Leighton would want to run away? Where do runaways go, and how do they survive? Is there anyone out there who cares? Lexi and her friends face these and other painful questions in CEDAR RIVER DAYDREAMS #26.

A Note From Judy

I'm glad you're reading *Cedar River Daydreams*! I hope I've given you something to think about as well as a story to entertain you. If you feel you have any of the problems that Lexi and her friends experience, I encourage you to talk with your parents, a pastor, or a trusted adult friend. There are many people who care about you!

I love to hear from my readers, so if you'd like to receive my newsletter and a bookmark, please send a self-addressed, stamped envelope to:

Judy Baer
Bethany House Publishers
11300 Hampshire Avenue South
Minneapolis, MN 55438

———

Be sure to watch for my *Dear Judy . . .* books at your local bookstore. These books are full of questions that you, my readers, have asked in your letters, along with my response. Just about every topic is covered—from dating and romance to friendships and parents. Hope to hear from you soon!

Dear Judy, What's It Like at Your House?
Dear Judy, Did You Ever Like a Boy
(who didn't like you?)

Live! From Brentwood High

Other Books by Judy Baer

9610

Teen Series From
Bethany House Publishers

—ԾԾ—

Early Teen Fiction (11–14)

HIGH HURDLES by Lauraine Snelling
   Show jumper DJ Randall strives to defy the odds and
   achieve her dream of winning Olympic Gold.

SUMMERHILL SECRETS by Beverly Lewis
   Fun-loving Merry Hanson encounters mystery and excitement in Pennsylvania's Amish country.

THE TIME NAVIGATORS by Gilbert Morris
   Travel back in time with Danny and Dixie as they ex-
   plore unforgettable moments in history.

Young Adult Fiction (12 and up)

CEDAR RIVER DAYDREAMS by Judy Baer
   Experience the challenges and excitement of high
   school life with Lexi Leighton and her friends—over
   one million books sold!

GOLDEN FILLY SERIES by Lauraine Snelling
   Readers are in for an exhilarating ride as Tricia Evan-
   ston races to become the first female jockey to win the
   sought-after Triple Crown.

JENNIE MCGRADY MYSTERIES by Patricia Rushford
   A contemporary Nancy Drew, Jennie McGrady's
   sleuthing talents promise to keep readers on the edge of
   their seats.

LIVE! FROM BRENTWOOD HIGH by Judy Baer
   When eight teenagers invade the newsroom, the result is
   an action-packed teen-run news show exploring the love,
   laughter, and tears of high school life.

THE SPECTRUM CHRONICLES by Thomas Locke
   Adventure and romance await readers in this fantasy
   series set in another place and time.

SPRINGSONG BOOKS by various authors
   Compelling love stories and contemporary themes
   promise to capture the hearts of readers.

WHITE DOVE ROMANCES by Yvonne Lehman
   Romance, suspense, and fast-paced action for teens
   committed to finding pure love.